BLACK, WHITE AND GREY

Best wishes.

Ashim Basnet

ASHIM BASNET

INDIA · SINGAPORE · MALAYSIA

Notion Press

Old No. 38, New No. 6
McNichols Road, Chetpet
Chennai - 600 031

First Published by Notion Press 2018
Copyright © Ashim Basnet 2018
All Rights Reserved.

ISBN 978-1-64429-642-4

This book has been published with all efforts taken to make the material error-free after the consent of the author. However, the author and the publisher do not assume and hereby disclaim any liability to any party for any loss, damage, or disruption caused by errors or omissions, whether such errors or omissions result from negligence, accident, or any other cause.

No part of this book may be used, reproduced in any manner whatsoever without written permission from the author, except in the case of brief quotations embodied in critical articles and reviews.

Dedicated to my hero, my late father

Dr. Bhim Singh Basnet.

*He taught me the power of simplicity, humility and integrity,
and above all, to find the good in everyone.*

Contents

Acknowledgments

First and foremost, I would like to thank my parents, Bhim and Prabha. I am what I am because of them, and there is no way in the world I can thank them enough for their unconditional love. I would also like to thank my two sisters Anupa and Anuja for their unfaltering love and support.

I am also highly obliged to my brother-in-law, Prajwal Khatiwada for his ever present support in everything I do, and specifically for being among the first to encourage me to put my stories on a paper.

I also thank my family members, all of whose names will not be possible for me to mention. I hope that each and every one of you will accept my gratitude and love.

What would life be without you, my dear friends? Cheers to each and every one of you. I would be failing in my duty if I don't mention a few names. Tenzin C. Tashi, Tashi Chopel, Ashish Sharma, among many, thanks for your encouragement and support.

I am also highly grateful to Pankaj Giri, who is himself a published author. Thanks for all your help, suggestions and support, and for explaining to me the intricacies of writing and publishing.

Notion Press for giving direction and smoothening the road in the journey towards publishing this book. Sneha, Manisha and the whole team, thank you very much.

This book is also for my other parents. Bharat Mohan Adhikari, my father-in-law, for being the person that he is, an inspiration to millions. Sabita Adhikari, my mother-in-law for always showering love and blessings upon us. Thank you.

Sudeep, Lima, Rohit and Liza, for accepting me as an elder brother. The little ones, Saanvi, Namami, Aditya, Manya and Aanya, my blessings and love for you all, always.

My life would have no meaning without my kids, Anant and Ahana. I want to thank them both; Anant for hating everything I wrote—it made me strive for more perfection, Ahana for loving everything I wrote—it gave me more inspiration. Love you both, unconditionally.

Lastly, I want to thank my life partner, my dear wife Luna for being a better half in the true sense. Thank you for picking up the pen every time I dropped it and making me continue on this journey, sometimes even forcefully. Without your love, this

ACKNOWLEDGMENTS

book would have remained incomplete, as would my life. Without you, this book would not have been possible.

To my readers, this book is mostly for you, for without you this whole voyage is fruitless.

Ashim Basnet

THE FRIENDSHIP

A huge mansion stood proudly in all its grandeur beside the main road. A high wall, fenced off with electrical wiring, interrupted a private road leading to the huge ornate gates of the estate. A guard stood vigil at the entrance like a polished mannequin displaying its wares.

The compound was huge; three luxury cars were parked randomly in the yard with space to spare for a few more. Chatter and laughter echoed from within, hinting at the revelry inside.

The great room was opulent and effused wealth. Four men sat on handmade leather couches, crystal glasses in hands, semi-circled around a huge fireplace. They all looked relaxed and at ease with each other, radiating friendship and camaraderie. Their faces were flushed from the heat of the fire and brandy. As was usual, the conversation took the turn towards politics and society.

"The problem of this country is bloody illiteracy. And, of course, the people are not cultured enough,"

Rathore said, taking a sip from his glass and staring at the dancing flames in the fireplace.

"Yeah, I agree. Otherwise, what's the difference between us and the west?" Thakur added, his long frame looking longer as he stretched his legs as far as they would go.

"Look at the bribes we have to pay to run our businesses. The whole bloody system is corrupt," Rana replied, looking pensively at his friend Sharma, a minister of the State.

"What can we do? Elections need deep pockets, unlimited money and we have no choice. No one is clean. You three have generations of properties left behind by your forefathers. What about the general population?" Sharma added, trying repeatedly to adjust himself in the huge deep couch that felt too plush for his comfort.

The four of them had been friends since their school days. Three of them were from aristocratic backgrounds and Sharma had joined them through a scholarship given by Rathore's father, the owner of this mansion. Sharma was not of their elite lineage, but the red light on his car somewhat qualified him for their august company.

A butler came with another round of brandy, bowing after each refill. The conversation continued.

"Look at all the filth outside. Our people have no civic sense at all. The whole country has become a huge garbage bin. We pray to the Ganges and dump our shit there; we are a country of contradictions and confusions. That is exactly why we are going nowhere. Bloody democracy..." Rathore hissed with anger, his eyes bloodshot by a concoction of anger, heat, and brandy.

"What do you suggest then? A dictator or a monarch...?" Sharma queried, waiting for an answer from the owner of the house.

"I suggest that you people use the tax payer's money for better use instead of just filling your own pockets," Rathore quipped, looking directly at Sharma, trying to annoy his guest and draw him towards a verbal duet.

"By the way, Rana, I have managed to clear the project you wanted from the ministry. It's going to cost you a donation to our party," Sharma told his friend with a smile, craftily changing the subject and turning the attention away from his challenger.

"What donation? Who the hell has been financing your bloody election campaigns for the last twenty years?" Rana shot back at Sharma, giving him a glare with a questioning look.

"Not for me. I would never take from my friends, but for the top; I have already committed. How else do you think the proposal got through?" Sharma shot back.

"Guys, I have come here to relax and not bloody talk business. I just want to chill out with my buddies.

So, please continue your business chatter some other time," Thakur spoke after a long gap, in a smooth tone, his demeanour betraying a laid-back attitude towards the challenges of life.

"Thakur...! You bloody don't need to talk business with all the royalties from your books pouring in non-stop, oh great author. Anyway... you are right, let's all relax and get drunk," Rana taunted him with a friendly nudge.

"So, Thakur, you bloody lucky bugger... you are a celebrity, swimming in money and still a bachelor with not a responsibility in life. I envy you, my friend... such a charmed life," Sharma supplemented.

"The grass is always greener on the other side, my friend. Everybody has their own share of problems; it's just how you take it. I simply ignore it until it goes away, as it usually does. In the meantime, I enjoy the finer things of life. What about you? A big shot and a lovely wife waiting for you at home... how lucky can one get?"

The four friends went down the memory lane of their alma mater, a subject on which none of them ever got tired. Lost in their world of shared memories, this could and would continue for hours on end. They looked back into their school days, each memory re-strengthening their bonds and bringing smiles to their faces.

The four of them were very different from each other, but their language and other small habits clearly indicated the similarities picked up from the same institute. The wives had attempted to join in a few times but soon swore that they would never again be a part of the same stories that bored them out of their wits. The four, however, always seemed to enjoy the stories, and the meeting insidiously became a strictly male-only affair. The men did not mind it a bit.

Finally, after midnight, the four friends separated with a promise to meet again, soon.

The next time they met, a fortnight had passed. The meeting this time was unplanned and lacked the lustre of its previous precedents. The early morning newspaper headlines had screamed, *"Minister Sharma shot! His bodyguards dead."* The news had led to frantic phone calls between the other three friends.

Sharma had been shot while campaigning. The Naxals were suspected, even though they had yet to claim the act. Sharma had always opposed the Naxals and always maintained that armed revolution was not a solution in today's world.

The three sat around the fire, nursing their brandies. "How is he now?" Rathore took the lead.

"In a coma and still very critical. I talked with Rani just a little while ago," Thakur announced solemnly.

At the mention of Rani's name, the three friends seemed to be lost in their thoughts, each as private as the other. Their rendezvous always had four of them, and only being three felt strange, like a missing tooth, amplifying the tragedy manifold. The three looked worried, which led to the drinks being consumed at a rate faster than usual. The sips surreptitiously turned to gulps, and eventually, even the butler shrugged and put the whole bottle on the table for them to self-serve. Rathore switched on the television set and surfed until he landed on a news channel...

"The Minister is still critical, and a hunt is still on for the terrorist group responsible..."

"This was bound to happen. I had warned him thousands of times not to go about trying to be a bloody hero in the Naxal areas. They had already attempted twice earlier. This time they got him," Rana said, taking a swig from his glass and motioning the butler for a refill. The butler complied with an extra courteous bow.

"Sharma will be Sharma, always at the wrong place, but he has guts," Rathore kept the conversation going.

"What do you mean by always being at the wrong place?" Rana intercepted.

"Well, he studied in our school, did he not? It was not a place for him. He always thought that he deserved it and acted as if he was of our class," Rathore blurted, his speech impaired by the increasing alcohol in his blood.

"What has bloody class got to do with it? He got in fair and square through scholarship and always topped the class. This is not the time to berate him, for God's sake! He is fighting for his life. We grew up together and he is our dear friend," Thakur replied.

The room became quiet, highlighting the shadows dancing to the tune of the fire in the fireplace.

The three of them had bullied Sharma in the beginning, but eventually one by one had given up when they realized that they could not bully Sharma's spirit. Sharma's tenacity had forced them to accept and eventually befriend him. They had been inseparable since then, which had somewhat continued to date.

Rathore beckoned for more drinks, looking more aggressive by the minute. "You all are the least ones to sympathise with him. I know the truth. Rana, you use him for your business and Thakur—" Rathore raised his voice but was interrupted by Thakur.

"You are way too drunk and don't know what you are saying. Don't say things which you will regret later. He is our friend."

"Bullshit... our friend. He never was and never will be one of us. It takes generations to reach our status. It's only because of his post that you all humour him. At least have the courage to admit the truth. And Thakur, what about you? I know you hate his guts... Rani..." Rathore shouted, his speech blurry now.

"Don't bring her in between. This has got nothing to do with her," saying that, Thakur got up, taking up a threatening posture instinctively.

"Guys, I think we have had enough drinks for one night. Let's have dinner," Rana said, trying to defuse the situation delicately.

The friends had had fights before, in different permutations and combinations between them. Some of those had even led to bloody fisticuffs. But that had been quite some time back, in their younger days. Their friendship had passed through thick and thin and had stood the test of time.

The three friends sat at the dining table quietly, the atmosphere sombre. Rathore was completely drunk and was having difficulty even sitting straight and eating. Rana finally motioned the butler to take his master to his room and hand him over to his surely irate wife while the two of them continued their nibbling. Their hunger somehow did not match up to the lavish spread on the table.

"He is just drunk and did not know what he was saying. He is upset about Sharma being shot and cannot face the reality. You know he is a softie from the inside," Rana spoke softly, more to convince himself.

"No. He meant each and every word... It was from his heart. Truth forced out by the drinks. He has always looked down at Sharma and cannot get over the fact that he is a big minister whereas he himself just lives off his ancestral property. He should have been the minister; God knows he tried hard enough. Being a writer, it's my job to understand the human psychology. Don't forget that I make my living off it," Thakur said with a smile.

The two friends left the mansion and headed towards the hospital to check on Sharma. Paparazzi, news vans, and cameras filled the compound. The cameras turned towards them as soon as Thakur, the famous author and columnist, was recognised. The two of them continued their walk inside, pushing through any queries from them. They reached the ICU floor, and Rani gave a weak smile, beckoning them.

"How is he now?" the two queried almost in unison.

"Still critical," Rani replied, tears welling up in her eyes. The three of them sat there for a long time, comforting each other with their silence.

"Rani, I think you should go home. You look totally worn out. We could take turns," Thakur said, throwing a soft smile at Rani.

"No, no... I can't leave him, not at this moment. Even if I go home, my mind will be here and I will be more worried. I want to be near him... I can manage. It's late so why don't you both go home? You can always come back in the morning. There are enough people here," Rani replied, making her stand clear.

"Rana, you carry on. I think I will stay for some more time; there may be enough people here but definitely not enough true friends. Your wife must be waiting for you. As for me, thank God I am my own master," Thakur made clear his intention.

"Yeah, I think it's a good idea. Give me a call in case you need me. I will be here in a jiffy." Rana turned towards Rani. "Rani, have you eaten anything? Or should I get you something? Should I send Rita to accompany you? Really... it will not be a problem at all." Saying that, Rana got up.

"Don't worry, that is exactly why I am staying back. What are friends for if not useful in trying times? And anyway, I have nothing else to do, no one to report to," Thakur replied softly.

The two of them sat quietly, the history between them perfectly buried in the sands of time, with only subtle awkwardness lingering on.

"Thank you," replied Rani, pouring a glass of tea from a flask and offering it to Thakur. Even the simplest act of drinking tea together brought back hordes of quashed memories between them.

"How are you holding on? Don't worry, everything will be fine," Thakur said, starting some sort of conversation to distract her.

"I am fine, I guess... It was such a shock to all of us, but I know he will be fine. He has to be fine," Rani said, looking heavenwards, more to assure herself than as a reply.

"Good, that's the spirit. Now you rest for a while, I am here if anything is needed," Thakur said, leaving the sofa for her to lie down on. He plopped down on a plastic chair placed on the opposite side.

The sight of Rani sleeping in front of him with her breast heaving in tune with her breathing made his heart flutter with longing. He tried to ward off his feelings, which he had managed to make perfectly inconspicuous over time, but it was harder than he thought. It was a fact that she had chosen Sharma over him, but he did not harbour any bitterness towards her. He had loved her like life itself, and for some time she too had loved him. Then Sharma had entered their lives with his intelligence and self-made attitude. He did not even know when she had perniciously become Sharma's. That was all history now. She still seemed to be in love with the fellow even after two decades.

He knew her life had not always been easy; it had taken a lot of hard work and time for Sharma to reach where he was today. They had struggled for quite some time and had even gone through rough patches of poverty, but ultimately they had made it. He was a good and clean politician and had a strong bonding with his voters. Sharma had always been sincere and hard working. In school, too, it had taken them a long time to corrupt him enough to enjoy their company. Thakur, on the other hand, had been a laid-back person with no real ambition and liked to enjoy his life.

Rani had initially fallen for his style, but women almost always crave for more. He was a good boyfriend material but not good enough for a husband. He too had had ambitions but not the stereotype ones, and domestication was not in his blood one bit. Rani had slowly rejected him and his idiosyncrasies and bet on a safer horse. In his heart, he knew that she still had some passion for him. Sharma was just more convenient.

The dawn was just breaking, and mild brightness painted the sky outside. As he opened his eyes, he could see Rani staring at him with her dark deep eyes and a big smile on her lips. His heart raced as he smiled back... déjà vu.

"Thank you for supporting us in this hour of need, for being such a dear friend. The doctor just told me that he is out of danger, thank God," she said, her voice ringing with relief and happiness, tears flowing down her cheeks, undoubtedly tears of joy... of relief.

He was not her friend; he could never be her friend. Her friendship was something that he was never going to accept, it was never going to be enough.

"Great... I told you everything was going to be fine. When did I fall asleep? What time is it?" Thakur said, getting up to restore his blood circulation and to avoid her gaze lest he betrayed his thoughts.

"It's nearly six in the morning. They are going to let me meet him now. Why don't you go home to rest and come back later? You too look very tired," Rani told him.

"How can I go before I see him? No, I too want to meet him before I go... if it's fine with the doctors and you," Thakur asked.

"Of course... I am sure he would be very happy to see his friend."

As soon as Rani came out from the room, Thakur entered the room guarded by two uniformed policemen standing at the door. A private room had been converted into a makeshift ICU for security reasons.

Sharma looked frail, tubes running out of his body. It had been a miracle of sorts. Three bullets had been taken out of his body, each one missing the vital organs by one-hundredth of a millimetre. His security men had first taken most of the bullets, and three of his men were dead. When you are destined to live, you are destined to live, and not even bullets can harm you.

Sharma was conscious and a weak smile formed on his face as Thakur entered the room. Thakur sat on the steel tool beside the bed and clasped his friend's hand between his own.

"I am glad you are back... for a moment there you had us scared," was all he whispered to his friend.

Shortly, Thakur took leave of Rani, who repeatedly thanked him. Suddenly she seemed more alive, as if life had just returned to her bloodstream. He heaved a sigh and left. As soon as he exited the building, the cameras surrounded him and questions flew in from all directions. He decided to talk to the media—it would be good publicity for his upcoming book. "I have just met the minister, and as of now, he is out of danger. I am sure the hospital will officially endorse that. Thank you." Then, he took a crisp turn and walked away.

A black car came around the corner, and he got in. He was tired and sore and longed for a warm bath. He had left his car at Rathore's last night and would collect it later in the evening; maybe even have a couple of drinks. Drinks and food were things that Rathore never ran out of; he was a wonderful host.

The car slowly turned away from the city and headed towards the highway, its speed increasing. Thakur fell asleep as tiredness crept over him. The car suddenly swerved, leaving the highway, and turned towards the forest, jolting him awake. After driving for about an hour, the car halted near a small path that led into the forest. Thakur got down, looked around, and entered the forest. After a few miles of walking, two armed men escorted him further into the labyrinth of the jungle. After a while, a clearing came into sight with tents scattered around. As he entered the camp, everybody got up and stood in attention.

Thakur had worked really hard and had deviously managed to convince the villagers to fight for their rights; he was a part of the armed revolution. In fact, he was the head of the revolution in the area. He had seen the system fail the people, giving birth to frustrations and thus people were ready to be moulded into revolutionaries. It was actually a social problem with a social solution. The administration tried to suppress the revolution by force, not understanding the root cause of it all. It was all the better for him, as every day more people joined his force.

He had actually been researching for his first book when he got involved. It was his revenge against his love; it was his way of being a self-made man. The writing soon became his cover. There too he had been successful. He felt proud of himself—these simple people would follow him to death and he wielded tremendous power. Of course, many times one's personal interest could be covered in the guise of an act of revolution, which made him even more powerful. He enjoyed this power; it was like being a superhero, his identity hidden from the world. He loved the double life he led; it suited his character, a true leader. This was his identity, his destiny...

He would get him one day... and then Rani.

He faced his audience, "Comrades..."

THE MOMOS

The winter air was crisp and cold. Children blew hot steam from their mouths, simulating smoking. People basked in the warmth of the sun, soaking in the heat that seemed to defrost their frozen bodies, layer by layer. The sky was clear, as clear as it gets in the winter. Time seemed to drag along slowly, mesmerized by the beauty of the mountains around.

Hari was in a hurry, as always. He had been working in the small restaurant since he was eight. It was not a restaurant per se; it was more of a Deli selling momos. It was five years since his uncle had brought him here. His uncle had gone back to the village and left him here to survive on his own. His father had been killed by a bear in the jungle and his mother... he had no memories of her. People said that she had died while giving birth to him. Now he had no one left except his uncle—Kaka. It was now maybe three years since he last saw his old Kaka. He had nowhere to go, but life was not so bad.

It was already six in the morning, and the customers would be here in the next hour. Their restaurant served the best momos, and Hari was the specialist.

"Where have you been, you idiot? Who is going to knead the dough... your grandfather?" shouted Tashi the proprietor.

"The meat shop just opened; it seems the meat came in late, so I had to wait," Hari replied meekly. He immediately started the kneading, filled the steamer with water, and set it on the gas burner.

Generally, Tashi was good to him, apart from the occasional berating he gave during the rush hours when he lost his cool. Hari had a roof over his head and a belly full of food with money to spare. What else does a man need? He had been collecting money since the day Tashi paid him his first salary and until date had amassed a wealth of about ten thousand rupees.

Whenever he was free, he would take out the bundle and count aloud for Tashi and the other helper to hear. On many occasions, his boss had rounded off the amount by filling in the gaping deficit by an extra ten or twenty. Tashi was a decent person and was good to him, good enough to be precise.

The other helper Suk was from around the area but was not a fulltime employee. He would come early in the morning and leave in the afternoon, leaving the whole burden on Hari for the night, but he did help them tide over the peak hours. The cold drove most of the customers home early, and by six there would only be one or two occasional visitors. They closed by seven anyway.

The restaurant itself was Hari's residence, and at night after downing the shutters, he would have the whole setting to himself. He was the boss then. He could do whatever he wanted, and in a way, it was his home even if it was only during the night hours.

Tashi lived nearby in a small house with his wife Dicki. The couple had no children even after a decade of marriage. Sometimes they would invite Hari to their kitchen. Other times they made him cook whenever the occasion demanded, be it a party or any other function. Tashi would compensate him, and it supplemented his growing savings. Boarding and lodging being on the house, Hari hardly had any expenses.

Tashi entrusted the kitchen to him with little interference. Suk had resigned himself to being a helper second to Hari, reluctantly at first, but gradually accepting his fate. He had been a helper when Hari had walked into the kitchen as a boy of eight. Hari was a hard worker and as years passed, he slowly won over his employer's confidence. It had ultimately resulted in Tashi appointing him the master of the kitchen.

"Hari, are the momos ready yet? The customer at table two has been waiting for almost half an hour," Tashi shouted over the counter, his voice carrying over to the kitchen through the steamy air.

"Just five more minutes," shouted back Hari, speeding up his movements and issuing instructions to Suk who had to double up as a waiter. Tashi entered the kitchen, indicating the rush hour. During the rush hours, Tashi usually pitched in, trying to relieve some tension from the kitchen. By about three in the afternoon, they were free to take a breather before again enacting the same routine for the evening.

Tuesday was a day off in his part of the town and Hari had the freedom to indulge in whatever he pleased. He mostly enjoyed rising late. He ate lunch and caught a movie or strolled around the main market, just enjoying his day of freedom. He also met some people, who, like himself, worked in the several restaurants and had a day off too. Over a cup of tea, the conversation usually centred on their employers or their respective salaries. Many people would recognise him, and he would be desperately trying to place them. Plenty of customers visited the restaurant, and Hari's momos were gaining popularity with every passing day.

One Tuesday, as he loitered around the market, a man called out his name. The man was tall and fat, making him look overbearing. Hari didn't recognise him. "Hey boy... come here," the man shouted, waving his hand. Hari walked towards him, looking behind to make sure that it was him who was being beckoned.

"You... the Momo boy," the man confirmed his invitation.

"Yes, sir," Hari said, unsure of what the man wanted from him.

"I love your momos," the man said. "You have the touch, a gift. Come, let's have lunch. It's my treat." The man put an arm around Hari's shoulder. Hari was delighted to be invited to lunch by a fan of his cooking. It felt good. The man led him to a small restaurant that looked posh compared to the one he worked in.

"How long have you been working for Tashi?" the man said, indicating his acquaintance with his employer.

"Five years... Nearly six," Hari replied over a plate of rice and chicken curry.

"So, are you happy?" the man asked.

"Yeah... Tashi sir is very good to me," Hari replied, wondering where this conversation was heading.

"Have some more chicken," the man said, putting some more chicken on Hari's plate. "So, how much do you get paid?" the man asked, trying to sound as casual as possible.

"Enough..." Hari said, putting a hand over his plate.

"What?" the man asked, surprised.

"Enough chicken... I am full," Hari replied, trying to avoid the question.

For some time, the two concentrated on their plates. The conversation somewhat stalled until the man looked up and said, "If ever you want to leave Tashi, come to work for me. I will double whatever he is paying you. Maybe even give you a partnership. Imagine owning a part of the restaurant—it is a chance of a lifetime. Think about it."

The man paid for the food and walked away, leaving a confused Hari standing alone. He stood for some time, shook his head as if to dislodge a bad thought from his mind, and continued his window-shopping. He had planned to watch a movie but it was too late now. So he just loitered around the market area before he concluded his outing and headed towards his abode. Although the road was downhill, making his journey back somewhat easier, he was tired and the thought of work the next day, dampened his spirits.

***

Life went on in a cycle, round and round, the tracks leaving behind sagging skins and receding hairlines. It was now twenty years since Hari entered the employment of Tashi. Hari had aged beyond his years, and making momos was just a reflex to him now as is breathing. In... out... in... out. Hari's momos were in great demand now, and the orders he received were beyond any human's capabilities. Suk was dead, mercifully released from life and momos. Hari had four helpers now, and the restaurant had almost tripled in size. Tashi had gone quite old and hardly ever came to the restaurant. It was all Hari's show, except that the money went to fill Tashi's coffers. After his wife's death, Tashi seemed to have stopped taking any burden except occasionally coming to the restaurant to show proof of his existence and ownership.

Now and then Hari still remembered the offer the man had given him. He wondered why he had not given it a second thought. Maybe he was scared then to go out of his comfort zone, or maybe he had not believed the man. He had surely missed a chance given by destiny. Now it was too late, and he would always be a slave to Tashi. Hari often regretted the decision taken a long time ago. He sometimes cursed himself, cursed his lack of courage to grab the chance of a lifetime. He could have had his own restaurant by now, could be working for himself and not for someone else... someone, who did not even care.

"Shit..." Hari shook his head, trying to dislodge the regret welling up in his head. He was sick of the same, monotonous life. He missed his home. He did not even know if he had any relatives living. Surely the old Kaka was dead. Could his children be there? "What have I to show for all the bloody hard work I put in all these years? Not even someone to call my own," Hari said to no one in particular. Biren, one of the helpers looked at Hari and then continued to knead the dough.

"Hari... Hari... where the hell are you?" Tashi shouted over the din in the restaurant. Hari came out of the kitchen, surprised to see his boss after a long time.

"*Agya*, what is wrong? Why are you here? I would have come to the house," Hari said in a hurry, calling Tashi *Agya*, a gesture of respect in the Tibetan community.

"Come to the house at night. I have called some people over to play cards. Cook something nice for us," Tashi said before turning around and walking off.

***

Four friends sat cross-legged in a circle on the carpet. Three decks of cards were mixed and twenty-one each distributed—they were playing marriage, a card game. The house looked dirty with cobwebs strategically placed all around. The cleanliness seemed to have died with Dicki. Dicki the barren, she could not give Tashi his heir, the prince for the momos... left him with only Hari.

"*Agya*, the dinner is ready," Hari announced, looking at the clock on the wall where both its hands pointed upwards indicating midnight.

"Shut the hell up... and get us a bottle," Tashi slurred, staring at Hari with bloodshot eyes.

"But... but it is late, and I got to start early tomorrow," Hari rebutted softly.

"To hell with you and your momos... get me a fucking bottle. Here, take these keys and bring some money from inside," Tashi said, handing over a set of keys.

"But Agya, you get it yourself. I don't want to have anything to do with money. Dicki Madam always told me not to enter the bedroom," Hari said, reluctantly taking the keys.

"Just shut up and do what I tell you, you shit. I am the boss of the house now."

Hari slowly opened the door to the bedroom, removed his shoes, and stepped inside. It felt like entering Dicki's sanctuary, his feet guiltily sliding across the wooden floor. His eyes adjusted to the dim light reflecting from a *diya*, the light flickering now and then. His eyes searched for the safe and finally stopped at one corner where the safe was sitting. He turned the keys and opened the door to the safe.

There were stacks of notes haphazardly stuffed inside and jewellery glistening against the flickering lights. Hari's eyes flew wide open as he covetously scanned the loot. He could feel all the years of his labour collectively stacked over each other. Each item represented his sweat, his early mornings, his late nights, the scolding, the fighting, and the bargaining. He picked up a wad and swiftly closed the safe shut, his hands shivering.

Finally, at about two in the morning, Tashi and his guests had their dinner, all drunk. The guests slowly took their leave, cue for Hari to clean up and leave.

Hari slowly closed the main door, the only entrance to the house. It clicked shut from inside.

***

It was nearly dawn. He walked briskly past the restaurant, and then he walked on and on until by daylight he had reached the outskirts of the town. By now, it was time to open the restaurant—the boys would be waiting. Hari found a truck going downhill, waved at it, and hitched a ride. It was nearing afternoon when the truck reached the hustle bustle of a border town. He handed the driver some money and made his way across the border as if disappearing into the darkness.

***

Back in Gangtok, Tashi was being carried out... only, he was dead. Dead... his throat slit. A neat cut across the throat with surgical precision. A cut made by the hand of a person used to cutting meat every day. The boys were all there, the police questioning them. The name "Hari" could be heard repeatedly in the police station, but no one knew where Hari was, where he was from, or even if it was his real name.

***

Hari slowly walked uphill, whistling a tune that he had heard on the radio, his breathing rapid due to exertion. The bag on his hand swayed, burdened with a heavy weight. A path was leading uphill through the jungle. Hari breathed hard, out of practice of walking in the mountainous path, his feet now strangely unsure in the narrow path through which he used to run when he was a small child. Some vague subconscious memories led him through the trail, and as he progressed, the cobweb of his mind slowly cleared.

The path gradually dipped down and turned towards the river. There was a bamboo bridge across it, and a small hamlet could be seen perched on the hilltop. Hari stopped to catch his breath and take a drink of the cool water from the stream. There was no one around, the area being sparsely populated. He rested the bag delicately on the ground just beside the flowing water and sat for a while before opening the bag.

There were bundles of notes, gold, and jewellery. Hari had grabbed some papers in the dark too while Tashi's blood made the bed sheet go red and then purple. "He was too drunk... he did not know," Hari told the soft wind blowing over the swaying bridge, wiping away his perspiration. He separated the sheets of paper and wondered what they were. Hari could not read. He looked at the papers for a long time, closed the bag, got up, and started walking across the bridge. As he reached the centre of the bridge, a huge smile on his face, he threw the papers into the flowing water and walked on.

The papers scattered over the flowing water, and within moments, the currents swiftly took them away.

A paper floated for some time before reaching a rapid and smashing against the stones. A part of it came up again.

"I, Tashi, in sound health and mind do hereby leave all my property including my Momo shop, a house, money in the bank, and all that is legally owned by me to Hari..."

THE OLD MAN AND THE YOUTH

It was very early in the morning, and a few dogs lingered about the otherwise empty Gangtok bus stand. The chill air of the night was just about dissolving with the rising sun. The old man lay wheezing, the chill working up a bout of cough that made him cower with breathlessness—a daily episode that eventually diminished as the day progressed.

The old man looked around for a tea vendor, but he could not find one; it was still too early. He had to go to Siliguri, and the bus left from Gangtok, about an hour's drive from his village. A few jeeps plied to the city from his village, the timings erratic, depending upon the whims of the drivers and their nightly quota of *rakshi*—a traditional distilled alcoholic beverage. He had to reach Siliguri today, no matter what. That had compelled him to sleep overnight in the bus station lest he did not get transportation so early from his village.

In the early days, he would not have had to sleep in the bus stand at all. All the old-timers he knew were gone, and their posterity no more welcomed an old rustic from the village to their homes. Gangtok had changed, for better or worse, who was he to question? The buildings were taller and the hearts smaller. Now people looked at him with disdain and even with suspicion. He did not like coming to the city anymore. But today he had to reach Siliguri, and the only way was through Gangtok.

It was nearing five-thirty now, and the bus would leave at seven. He had to freshen up and get some tea. Ah, tea, it was one of his vices, not *rakshi* or cigarettes... his poison was tea or so his wife told him. He needed tea almost every hour. He liked the fragrance and the taste of tea and without it, he was but a cranky old man. But today he pushed himself up without his customary cup of tea in bed. At home, his wife would not dare wake him up without a cup in her hands, even if she was dying.

Luckily, no one had disturbed him during the night like the last time, except a stray dog that had snuggled up against his back and slept. He had initially thought of chasing it away, but the warmth it gave his sore back stopped him from doing anything like that. When he woke up, the dog had gone its own way. Thanks to it, his back was less sore even though it took some time for him to get all his parts mobile. From petrol to a diesel engine, that is what age had done to him. He needed heating up before he could start his day, especially in winter, and the older he got the longer it took him.

He knew his way about, this being not his first night in the city. He had some money with him, but he didn't wish to waste it on a hotel when he could get a perfectly good night's sleep here. The money would go a long way in Siliguri, and he could afford the rice and *Cheetal-Peti*, the stomach portions of the Clown knifefish he so loved; otherwise he would have to make do with only *Rohu*, the cheaper fish. Another vice of his—food. He loved his food, especially of the non-vegetarian variety. Some people eat to live while some live to eat; he sure was of the latter type. What was life without a little passion, tea, and meat... and of course the occasional drink of the other type?

The old man completed his morning ablutions just as a tea vendor opened his shop. It was nearing six, and finally, he was getting a cup of tea. The old man cradled the cup in his hands and took occasional sips, relishing the sweet amber liquid, a wide grin plastered on his face. Only he could understand the importance of that bloody liquid for his body. It was like a dose of life-saving medicine for the gravely infirm. Every sip reinforced his faith in God and the overall good of humankind. He reluctantly took the last sip and handed back the chipped cup to its rightful owner along with the charges accrued.

The ticket counter would open at around half past six, and as was usual with him, he was the first in line.

Slowly, a few potential travellers started queuing up behind him. The old man stood smugly at the head of the line, the feeling of being first in line washing over him, adding to his arrogant stance. The counter finally opened, and the teller was busy arranging his paraphernalia for the ensuing sale of tickets. As the man behind the counter looked at the old man, suddenly, a young man dressed in tattered jeans and a T-shirt with a jacket tied around his waist appeared out of nowhere, and without acknowledging the queue, shoved his hand inside the counter with the requisite fare.

For a moment, the old man was stunned before he uttered, "I am first... I have been waiting since last night." The youth looked at the old man and pushed him roughly, the tattoo of a snake coiled around a cross on his arms clearly visible as the sleeves of the T-shirt shifted upwards. The old man, who had seen so many more suns than this young shit was not about to just stand silently. He shouted at the teller, "I was here first... What is this nonsense?" Then, looking at the young man, he shouted, "Young man, I am old enough to be your grandfather. Don't you know how to behave with your elders?" The old man looked around for support from other co-passengers, but no one uttered a word.

The young man again pushed the old man and said, "*Bajay*-old man, I am in a hurry and I am the youth convener of the ruling party. Don't you know that? So just shut up, otherwise, I may really get angry."

Everybody kept quiet. The teller gave the ticket to the young man, and as he walked away, he told the old man, "Don't worry, all of you are going to reach at the same time. It's not like he is going to reach there faster just because he got the ticket first."

"It's not about getting there first. It's about your right and respect. I was here first, and I should have got the ticket first. The current generation has no respect for us elders. What is happening to our society and today's world? How can he push me? I am old enough to be his grandfather. Such people have no right to live in this world… I curse him."

"Don't take him too seriously. He is just a local goon and a bully. I have given you a window seat, so just relax and enjoy your journey."

"I guess you are right. It's just that it was really humiliating being bullied by someone as young as my grandson. You know my grandson is in the army, and I am going to Siliguri to receive him."

The old man slowly rolled up his blanket and put it in his bag. He sat down for some time, the bitter incident still gnawing at his heart. He took a long breath and started chanting the *Gyatri* mantra. The mantra always soothed him, but not today. Deep inside, he still cursed the uncouth youth. He wanted such people to be wiped out from the face of this earth.

As he entered the bus, he could see the fellow sitting just behind his seat, on the aisle side. He could see the haughty smirk on his face as if he was the lord and all others his slaves. The old man avoided the look the idiot gave him and quietly sat on his seat. A young girl came and sat adjacent to him.

The journey started without any other untoward incident. The bus started slowly, flowing with the heavy traffic that seemed to have engulfed Gangtok these days. In his days, there was hardly any traffic on the road, and the highway was, in fact, an extension of one's boundary. There would be children playing and pickles and carpets spread out to dry right in the middle of the road. The occasional vehicle would pass through apologetically, as if it was the trespasser on the road and not vice versa. Now, one could see a beeline of vehicles extending until the end of the world and the air thick with smoke and dust. No wonder that the Gangtokians always looked sick and irate.

The bus gradually started to gain momentum as it left the city behind and the trees whizzed past at an increasing speed. Slowly, all the passengers settled down and found their own tempo of comfort. Some looked outside at the serene hills and the water flowing in the Teesta River alongside the road, others just dreamt with their eyes open, and some others dozed off, their bodies swaying with the rhythmic contour of the road.

The old man looked out of the window, enjoying the fresh air streaming through the window. He aligned himself with the wind flow and adjusted his body into a comfortable yet awkward posture that was sometimes required in a government bus seat. The boy leaned forward on the aisle side and started talking with the girl beside the old man. The banter mixed with young laughter that could be heard over the roaring engine gladdened his heart. He tried to eavesdrop on the conversation, but he finally gave up, the topic being beyond his comprehension, and slowly drifted away into a light slumber.

Suddenly the old man was rudely shaken awake. The uncouth youth was standing over him, still shaking him as he opened his eyes. "*Bajay*, you sit behind on my seat—as it is you are sleeping. l am going to sit here so that we can talk easily," the youth said. The old man could not believe the insolence of the fellow. He simply refused to say anything and continued to sit on the seat. The youth stared hard at the old man and said, "*Bajay*, I am once again requesting you politely. I hope I don't have to force you. What the hell is the problem with you anyway?"

The old man lost his cool. Standing up, he started to shout at the young man, his face red with rage, "You bloody idiot, who do you think you are? Don't you have any respect for elders? Is this what your parents have taught you? If you want to sit here, you will have to kill me. If my grandson was here with me, he would have kicked the shit out of the likes of you."

Adamant, the old man continued to sit in his seat, the youth throwing obscenities at him from behind. The bus continued its journey amidst the dying protests of the youth who eventually quietened down after realizing that the old man would not budge. At their destination, the youth got down, purposely pushing the old man, before walking off. The old man stood outside the bus for a long time, trying to compose himself after the unpleasant ordeal. He was going to meet his grandson after a gap of one year, but the whole incident left a bitter aftertaste no matter however much he tried to compose himself.

By the time the rickshaw reached the New Jalpaiguri railway station, he was already half an hour late. The old man got down, paid the fare, and scanned the station area for his grandson. There was a lot of hustle and bustle, and people were swarming all over the place. At last, he saw his grandson emerge from within the station building, looking smart in his army uniform. The old man felt his chest swell with pride. He thanked the Almighty that his grandson was nothing like that uncouth youth.

His grandson saw him and increased his speed towards him. The old man stood still, all his worries and tension washing away as his grandson touched his feet and then hugged him tightly.

Suddenly, his grandson waved at someone with a big grin and said, "My best friend too has come to receive me."

Eager to meet his grandson's friend, the old man turned around. He froze in horror as he came face to face with the uncouth youth.

THE EVERLASTING FIGHT

She looked in the mirror and slowly turned towards an old photograph that hung on the wall. She vividly remembered the photo taken by her husband, some four decades ago; they had just got married then. She looked pretty, innocent, and happy. She once again looked into the reflection in the mirror and saw a hard face staring back at her. When had she changed so much, when had these hard lines contoured her face and turned her into someone so stern and unwelcoming? Well, life had been tough, life was tough and she had toughened up, especially so after her husband's death.

The only one she had was her son, Abhay, her only child. She had struggled to take care of him, to educate him, to put him through college, only to be stolen... stolen by a mere girl. What did the girl know about the sacrifices she had made? The bitch just swooped down and took him away, hunky dory. Tears formed in her eyes just thinking of her son. He was everything she had, and they had gone through so much together. Had he forgotten all that, had he forgotten his own mother? Had she sacrificed everything for this?

Dhanmaya combed rigorously, trying to smoothen the knots in her hair. The tangles disappeared as her anger dissolved and her tears dried, her white hair flowing like a river of silk, down until her knees. Her husband never let her cut her hair. "It's so lovely, don't ever cut it..." She could still hear her husband's voice in her head.

Dasai—or *Dussehra* as it is generally called, the autumnal festival celebrating the victory of good over evil—was just around the corner, and she had so much to do. There would be guests, hordes of them coming to put *Tika*—a blend of rice, vermillion and curd pasted on the forehead as a mark of blessings by the elders—from her. "Gauri... Gauriiiii," she shouted.

Gauri had been with her for forty years now, a dowry given by her father in her marriage. Servants were so hard to find these days, and Gauri was a blessing and almost a member of the family... almost. A servant is always a servant and can never be a member of the family, but Gauri was almost family. Dhanmaya still remembered her father's house. She would always be surrounded by servants then. Now, it was different. She lived alone, except of course for Gauri, if she could be counted. Her son, her only child, had gone, leaving her house empty.

Gauri had a worn out apron tied around her waist and held a broom in one hand. She too had grown old along with her mistress. "Gauri, clean the bedroom. You know *Bhai* is coming for *Dasai*," Dhanmaya said loudly to be heard over the growing deafness of Gauri. She sometimes suspected that Gauri feigned her deafness to avoid her instructions. The old bitch was as shrewd as a politician.

"But Memsahib, *Dasai* is still two weeks away," Gauri said. "If I clean it now, it will get dirty by the time *Bhai* arrives. Is he coming alone? What about Sunita memsahib?"

"Just do what I say," Dhanmaya barked. "Have I told you to use your empty head? Go right now and do some actual work instead of just dillydallying around as usual."

She had been only about twenty-five when on that dreadful night the police had come to her doorstep. Abhay was just three. "There has been an accident. We need you to come and identify the body." These simple words had crashed her world. She had been inconsolable for years, but she had to live on for her son. Her son had never known his father. Time heals everything... or does it? Tears would still flow whenever she thought of that night. They had been married for just five years when fate snatched him away, leaving behind an infant and an ailing mother-in-law.

As a young widow, she had understood why being one was considered one of the worst curses of life. There were always vultures around, trying to pounce on her, but she had been strong, and slowly the vultures disappeared over the years. She had to turn her heart into stone to deal with the world and to add to that her husband had left behind an extra baggage, an old baggage. No matter what she did, the old woman was never happy. "If only my son was alive... he would have..." she used to bicker almost every day.

But her son was no more, and Dhanmaya could only do so much. She really hated the old witch. Luckily for her, the witch was also no more. But despite all the abuses, she did miss her sometimes. More than herself, she missed her for Abhay—he simply used to adore his grandmother. She let out a huge sigh as the painful truth broke over her again. Abhay had gone, leaving her alone... all alone.

Dhanmaya slowly folded the day's newspaper and put it atop a heap that she would later sell to the *raddiwala*—the scrap collector. The idiot always tried to fool her, saying, "Madam I can only give you Rs. 5 per kg, and I give the best rates."

"Best rates my foot. I will give it for no less than Rs. 10 per kg," she would haggle customarily. Eventually, they always settled for Rs. 7 per kg, but the two of them liked to bargain as if it was a game. And a game it was—a tradition followed in almost all the households in her part of the world.

She remembered when she had told her son about the bride she had chosen for him. He had looked shocked. "Ma, I am only twenty-five, and I don't want to get married now. Give me some time," he had pleaded with her. The boy had ultimately agreed after a lot of emotional blackmailing by his mother. When the potential bride and groom met for the first time, she was pleased to see the young couple hitting it off almost instantaneously. After that, the boy had not needed any further convincing. Dhanmaya had been happy until then. Life had almost stopped kicking and punching her.

The marriage had been lavish, which she could afford then after years of toil. Who would have thought that her investments would work out? Had she been clever, courageous, or maybe just lucky? Sometimes simple courage was enough. Anyway, after her son's marriage, life was good. Her new daughter-in-law respected her, and her relation to Dhanmaya was the antithesis of Dhanmaya's own with her mother-in-law. She was at last happy, at last at peace... her work done, her responsibilities over. Now she could enjoy the fruits of her labour, her sacrifices.

***

It was her fault, she had chosen Sunita—her son had been against marriage from the beginning. Sunita was very sweet, or so she thought. Sunita was always courteous to her, but Dhanmaya had slowly realized that it was merely a façade. Beneath the fake niceness

41

lay a scheming bitch. From day one of the marriage, Abhay had changed and started following his wife like a puppy. All the years of her love and sacrifice had gone in a single puff, so easily forgotten by her own flesh and blood. Slowly, discussions and then arguments started between her and Sunita. Even the smallest of things would spark off a huge fire. Sunita wanted to be the boss of the house, and Dhanmaya was supposed to sit in a corner as if she was dead. Dhanmaya showed her, though, threw her out of her house. But who would have thought that her son would follow his wife like a dog? *That ungrateful fool*, she thought... but in a moment, longing dissolved the anger. She missed him... she missed him so much.

This *Dasai* they were coming home after a gap of three years, three years of solitude and loneliness, three years of waiting near the telephone for a single call from some place called Buffalo. Finally, the call had come, from her son. If she wanted, they would be home this *Dasai*... All the bottled emotions had boiled over, and she had cried like never before.

"Gauri, have you inquired about the mutton...? You know how much Abhay loves it. What about the beaten rice and the pickle... have you put it out in the sun?" Dhanmaya asked her loyal help.

"Don't worry, Memsahib, I have been in this house for a long time. I know what *Bhai* likes. You just relax," Gauri said in a loud tone.

"Now you idiot will teach me how to run this house...? Relax, my foot, my son is coming home after three years and you say relax? I am sure that is what *you* have been doing all day, you lazy bum," Dhanmaya shouted even louder as Gauri ran towards the kitchen, the abuses bouncing off her back.

Dhanmaya was tired... She was old and tired. Now, she did not have the energy to fight anymore. She had been fighting for decades, and now, she was tired. She had fought with the vultures, with her husband's cousins when they wanted their brother's share of the property, with her mother-in-law, with people wanting to cheat her, with her son's teachers when they bullied him just because he was fatherless. She had fought for almost everything. She was tired... she did not want to fight anymore, she wanted to be taken care of for a change, talked nicely to; she wanted to be loved, and mostly she wanted to be wanted. She had sacrificed so much. She deserved to be happy.

After her husband was gone, money had been the most important thing in her life. She needed money to survive, to give a life to her son and her mother-in-law. Her husband had left them very little. Without the security of her husband, she had realized the importance of money. Money was everything. Without it, there was no life, no happiness. So she had worked hard, and luck began to take her side in so much as to give them enough money. Enough, to dilute its own importance. Enough, so that she never had to think about it again. She had been happy, she and her son. Even the witch towards the end had started to respect her. Money gave her everything— happiness, respect, security.

Age... it is such a great teacher. Yet, it is so very cruel. It teaches you so much about life, the mistakes that you made. But it is so gradual that by the time you realize the mistakes, it's too late to do anything about it. It takes away your courage, your strength, slowly eating at it... eroding it until you have nothing but fear. Fear of everything, fear of the end... fear of dying all alone.

The last three years had made Dhanmaya realize so many things. Solitude had forced her to think, to analyse, and to realize. Three years had made her wiser, wise enough to install a bitter realization into her heart, a realization that in the end, money was nothing but false pride. She was scared. She did not want to be alone anymore. She wanted to be needed, to be loved, to be respected. That was what life was all about... at least at her age. She was ready to surrender unconditionally to Sunita, to swallow her pride, for being loved, for being wanted.

The Toyota Innova slowly crunched its way through the gravel driveway, coming to a slow halt just outside the main door. The atmosphere was filled with anticipation as if the gods were in the process of formulating a climax. Dhanmaya stood timidly at the threshold of the door, her heart palpitating in anxiety. Tears welled up in her eyes. The things she had planned to tell Sunita bombarded her mind. She was tired now and ready to hand over the reins of the house to her daughter-in-law. She had finally learnt the lesson that life had to teach.

One of the doors of the Innova slowly opened, and the smiling face of her son Abhay emerged. He gazed at her, tears running down his face. Her heart felt wrenched from inside. She waited for Sunita to come out as her son moved towards her, touched her feet, and hugged her tightly. All her troubles disappeared like the mist clearing with the heat of the sun.

The other door slowly opened, and Dhanmaya waited in anticipation for the move Sunita would make. A white woman came out. Dhanmaya sucked in air to control her shock. She looked at her son with questioning eyes.

"Ma, I wanted to tell you in person," he muttered. "Sunita left me about a year ago. I have married again... This is Sharon. She is an American."

Dhanmaya looked towards her new daughter-in-law, her eyes twinkling. Her gait changed from stoop to erect as if her bones had suddenly woken up. Her chest puffed out, and all the memories of Sunita diminished by the second. As Sharon walked towards her, an aura of pride enveloped Dhanmaya. She was once again the queen of her house. She was going to show this new girl her place in the house from the beginning itself. At least Sunita was of her own caste. This woman was nothing but a *Gori* who knew nothing about their culture, about respect. She was going to teach her.

Abhay looked at his mother, seeing how once again she was changing from the soft, accommodating mother to the hard, demanding mother-in-law. He knew what lay ahead. He sighed and shaking his head meekly, walked into the house...

THE PROJECT

"You can wake up a sleeping man but not someone who is pretending to sleep," Ranjit said aloud, as he read through the morning papers, blaming the Prime Minister for the dingy affairs of the state.

"The people have built this country and will have to continue doing so, in spite of our government," he said to no one in particular. Mr. Ranjit Sharma, a government officer, had just retired, and suddenly he had all the time in the world. He had retired as a Joint Secretary, a high official in the Central Government. He was a man of principles, liked and hated equally and posted repeatedly to the remotest parts of the country for his sincerity.

"I have been transferred fifty times in my career, fifty!" He said proudly to everyone as if showing off his scars of battle. He always talked about how corruption was ruining his country.

On the bright side, the postings had helped the family see up close the different corners of the country. It was a great education for their son, who had become tolerant and understood the diversity of the land.

The apartment had three bedrooms and was simple and comfortable. They had fallen into the habit of three bedrooms, like the official quarters in which they had been living over the years. It was on the first floor of this eight-storied building, a boon since the erratic power supply to the village often rendered the lift redundant. This flat was his whole life's earnings. His father had been a farmer and had somehow managed to support him through college. He had finally cleared the Indian Administrative Service and become an officer, the first from his village.

The flat was new, and he had just bought it from his retirement benefits. They had moved from the capital to their village, a seven-hour journey from the capital, a village in the foothills of the Himalayas, now slowly turning into a small shantytown. This was one of the new upcoming apartments.

"I have to go back tomorrow," Dilip said to his father, who seemed to be staring out of the window.

"No problem. We can manage now," he replied to his son's announcement. Dilip was an MBA and working in a multinational company, working against the people, as his father put it. There was silence for some time as both father and son were lost in their thoughts, adjusting to the new phase of their life.

The kitchen door opened, and a small petite woman came out carrying a dish, "Help me set the table. Dinner is ready," she said to both of them, hoping that at least one of them would be listening. Mrs. Sharma had lived for too long in a men only household and sometimes missed the gossip and lively talks of women, missed having a daughter. Dilip got up to help his mother, more out of hunger than willingness. His mother was a great cook and that was the one thing he always missed.

Mrs. Sharma usually had time to herself, and she needed tending to herself too. Her husband would be out of the house by eight in the morning. The rest of the day used to be hers to indulge in. Now, after his retirement, her husband would always be home with her. She had been dreading this day for years. She was as nervous as her better half was adjusting to this new tempo.

"Papa, now you are free to follow your passions," Dilip told his father, smiling.

"I was already following my passion, the passion to serve my country. Unlike you I have not sold my soul to the devil and work only for the money," Ranjit replied, trying to instigate his son into a debate.

"Why can't we be like a normal family and talk about normal things like the weather?" Devi said, serving the two of them, nipping the impending debate in its bud.

"It's not me, it's Papa, as usual. All he can talk about is his great country," Dilip replied before he started to tend to his hunger.

Dilip loved his father and admired his patriotism, but he wondered if it was enough for a country. His father had always been a leftist even though he denied it. "Socialism... that is what I believe in. There is too much gap between the rich and the poor," was always his defence. At home, Dilip always left the contrabands in his room, his Rolex, his Gucci, his Armani, lest his father start his lecture.

The father and son were two sides of the same coin; both loved their country; the difference was in their methods. One believed that everyone should earn equally, and the other believed that it should be left to individual capabilities, and eventually everyone will get their due. Both were right—it's never the system; it's always the intention of the people running the system that makes the difference.

A vital wealth had been passed down from father to son: integrity and strength, the icing on the cake being their love for the country. These very qualities had propelled Dilip up the ladder of the corporate hierarchy. He was a prodigy of his company and one of the youngest in its management. Ranjit was proud of his son but never expressed it in front of him, lest it inflamed his ego. Dilip was proud of his honest father, a rare blossom in the huge forest of corruption. Both did not let the other know.

Dilip left the next morning, contented at the first-hand knowledge of his parents' comfort. He drove his "Toyota Fortuner" through the rough lane of the village, leaving behind a train of dust to settle down. He thought of the debates he had with his father. His father was a dirty fighter and always used his age to his advantage. The respect he got from his son was his strongest weapon; he wielded it at the slightest provocation. Ultimately, the debate usually turned into a monologue with Dilip keeping his peace and listening to his father's lofty sermon quietly. He enjoyed giving his father the respect he deserved even though he did not always agree with his opinions.

Dilip stayed in an apartment in the capital provided by his company and would come back once a month to visit. He always felt that it was not enough and wanted to spend more time with his parents, but that was all he could manage in between his hectic corporate schedule.

***

The reality of retirement slowly started sinking in, and Ranjit basked in the sudden free time he had for himself. Devi too tried to set a routine that freed her from the attention of her husband for at least a few hours every day. Slowly, the married couple tried to adjust with each other for the second time in their lives, at leisure this time, unlike the hurried adjustment they had made in their youth.

Ranjit and Devi would talk for hours, making up for the lost time in their race of life. They would argue like newlyweds, a luxury they had been postponing for decades. The pulse of their remaining life was slowly being set up, supported by the knowledge of a son a mere phone call away.

The luxury of doing nothing is a luxury, but for a few days. After that, it slowly takes the form of boredom. Sixty is an awkward age, not old enough to be idle, not young enough to start anew. The mind is still sharp, but the body, just about beginning to be weighed down by age. Ranjit had felt that he could still have contributed much more even after the official retirement age. Gradually, monotony started to creep into his life—he had nothing to do. He had lived most of his life away from the village and had become totally disconnected. He had neither friends nor enemies here, and a person needs both to thrive. He missed the days when there were hundreds at his disposal. Most of the people here did not know him and the few that did, did not know about the contributions he had made for his country. He was a nobody here, no identity. He missed the power he had wielded, the respect he used to get. Here, he was simply a citizen without the cloak of power and position. He felt like a magician without a magic wand.

Ranjit sat down with a book 'Fountainhead' on a *charpoy*—a bedstead of woven webbing stretched on a wooden frame on four legs—spread out for his convenience on the terrace. He had always wished for time to read, and now that he had, he was going to utilize it to the fullest. After a few pages, his head started to droop with the weight of sleepiness. Devi came up to check on him and found him dozing.

"So that's what you have come to do," she said, trying to tease her husband.

"I was reading," he mumbled, his voice still thick with sleep. "I am tired, tired of doing nothing. Maybe I will go and watch some news for some time... don't have the habit of sleeping in the afternoon, I get acidity."

Ranjit collected his belongings, and the duo slowly walked downstairs. He watched the news for some time.

"Nothing interesting going on—rape, corruption, violence... bloody, the whole country is going down. It's the aftershocks of haphazard development and foreign influence. Globalization... bullshit, we were better off before," Ranjit mumbled to himself.

"If the news agitates you so much, why don't you watch something else?" Devi had a look of amusement on her face.

Ranjit surfed the channels, the luxury of DTH—crystal clear reception even in the interiors. A Hindi sitcom was on, and Ranjit watched it for some time, gradually getting engrossed, unsuspectingly.

Devi joined him. "*Aree*," she said. "You are watching this! I like it too. We can watch it together." But before she could further elaborate, Ranjit switched the channel. Ranjit had liked it but could not declare it in order to avoid the expected mockery from his better half.

The next day, Devi had gone to the temple. Ranjit put on the sitcom and watched with growing fascination. He was so engrossed that he did not hear his wife walk in. "Ranjit..." shouted his wife as she came out of the washroom. Ranjit hastily changed the channel when he heard his wife.

"What are you watching... fashion TV?" she alleged.

"What...? Not at all," Ranjit said, the models walking the ramp, the lingerie-clad bodies moving to the blaring music on the screen.

"You talk against globalization... but watch fashion TV," Devi said seriously, just about controlling the giggles building up in her stomach. Ranjit turned crimson red, for the first time in her life Devi had seen the thick-skinned bureaucrat blush.

Eventually, Ranjit openly started to watch the series and became somewhat of a TV worm. He started adjusting his life according to the demands of his TV schedule. His timings became weirder and weirder and it destroyed the somewhat logical routine of their life. The meal times changed from time to time, and the waking and sleeping times got juggled. Even his mood started to simulate the nature of the programme he just witnessed, tragedy—sad, comedy—happy, crime—suspicious.

"Devi did you steal money from my wallet," he asked one day, looking suspiciously at his wife.

Devi did not know what to do with the person who looked like her husband but had the personality of a stranger. When he was not watching TV, he was constantly nagging. His whole energy was now focussed on her and the apartment.

A wife dreams of complete attention of her husband her whole life, but when she actually gets it fulltime, it's a nightmare. 'Too much of anything tastes bitter' is, as the saying goes, quite true.

One morning Devi woke up to find the other side of the bed empty. Surprised, she called out to her maid. "Kantabai, have you seen sahib...? Where has he gone so early in the morning?"

Kantabai pointed upwards with one hand and covered her smile with the other. Devi rushed up to the terrace to find her husband washing his clothes.

"What is wrong with you...? Leave that and go down immediately," she shouted at her husband.

"Why can't I wash my own clothes...? You have been washing it for me for years," he replied calmly.

"What will people say...? This is a village, and people talk about small things. Just go down." She took the dripping garments from his hand and pushed him away. "And by the way, we do have a washing machine, you know."

To Devi's horror, he had started to show interest in the running of the household, her sacred domain. "Kantabai has not cleaned the floor properly today," he said, pointing under the sofa. He had never noticed such things before in his life and had left it to his wife. He started hanging around the kitchen, even trying to help his exasperated wife and a bemused servant.

Devi started to get up earlier to finish cooking before her husband entered her kitchen. "He has lived his life, and now he is trying to live mine," she used to tell Kantabai, who looked on, speechless. Devi felt like she was once again living with her mother-in-law. God, she had already done her time... not again!

"Devi, look, there are cobwebs in the cupboard," Ranjit said one day. Devi ignored him for some time.

"Why don't you go visit Dilip for a few days?" she replied finally. "He would be happy."

"He will be here after a few days anyway. Why should I go all the way?"

"*Arree*... you can catch up with your friends. They are all not dead, you know. Retirement means that you have only stopped going to the office, it does not mean you have to stop living, you know."

"Forget it; I have worked hard all my life. I want to relax for some time. Stop nagging me, woman."

Devi was at her wit's end; her husband was turning into a nightmare. The person who wanted to take on the world had now become, under the guise of retirement, his own antithesis.

"For God's sake, please go meet your relatives. Go meet Kaka," she said in a harsh tone.

"And talk about what...? They treat me like an outsider as if I am not from the family, the village," he whined like a child.

In life, a person's mannerisms are directly dependent on the current environment. Remove a person's anchor—be that his job, power, wife, passion, money, anything—and the person becomes someone different. For Ranjit, until now his life had revolved around his job, his power. Without it, he was like a cut kite. A kite which when held down by a thread soars skyward; cut the line and let it loose for it to fly higher, and it free-falls towards the ground, anti-logic. Everybody needs that line. Without it, our character, our personality takes a complete turnaround.

And so it was with Ranjit. Slowly, Devi was grudgingly taking on the role of the man of the house. Ranjit was becoming everything he was not.

***

A few days later, Devi was pleasantly surprised when she found a man standing outside the main door, ringing the doorbell. She asked him to come in.

"Ranjit, someone is here to see you," Devi shouted over the noise of her grinding machine. She had now started to grind her own spices unlike before when they used the readymade ones. These were the advantages of living in a village—fresh food, clean air, peace, and safety. What more could one ask for?

Ranjit hurried out of the room, pleasantly surprised that someone wanted him. An old man was squatting on the floor as if on a morning ritual. He got up and bowed as soon as he saw Ranjit.

"Sahib, I heard that you were a big sahib in the city. We need your help," he said, confident that this was indeed the right place.

"I am retired. I don't think I will be of much help," Ranjit replied.

"You are still alive, aren't you? You still have your brain and your contacts, don't you?" a sharp repartee came from behind the kitchen door.

"Sahib, a big project is being planned, and all our farms will be destroyed. Your lands too will be taken away. You have to help us. The land is all we have. It is our identity, our destiny," the old man pleaded. "Where are we to go?"

Ranjit kept quiet for some time. Devi came in, bringing two cups of tea. "Is this not where you were born, is this not where you have your roots, is this not why you wanted to come back here to live, away from the comforts of the city?" Devi said accusingly. "We could have stayed with Dilip. There is enough space in his apartment, and he is alone. But no... you wanted to come back to your village and serve the people here."

Ranjit kept his silence, pondering about what his wife had just said. She had wanted to stay on in the capital with her son. Dilip had pleaded with both of them.

"My place is with my roots, my people. What use is my education if I cannot use it for the good of the people?" had been Ranjit's defence. His wife had then supported him, to their son's dismay.

"Give me some time; let me think about it... Please come after a few days," Ranjit said, dismissing the old man.

***

Dilip was back home after a month. He looked happy to see his parents after a long gap. He had taken a week off to relax after the hectic month. "So what's new with both of you?" he asked as a formality.

"Oh, nothing new, just passing our time, our free time," Ranjit replied, looking at his wife.

Suddenly he blurted out, "By the way, your mother has become a nag and does not let me enjoy my retirement."

"Your father thinks he has become useless as if after retirement life is over. As far as nagging is concerned, God is the witness," Devi said softly, just about keeping her cool.

"It's not only that. Now that I don't have a job, no one respects me," Ranjit added.

Dilip listened silently to the two of them accusing and counter-accusing each other, trying to comprehend the situation, which was confusing to him. He kept his mouth shut lest it takes the shape of him taking sides.

After some time, quiet reigned, and trying to restore back the balance, Dilip said, "By the way, I have to go to France for a year. I hope you both can take care of yourselves until I return."

Again, no one spoke. The silence was icy cold, and time came to a standstill inside the room.

"You are not leaving us and shifting to France for good, are you?" Devi asked her son, a bit worried, tears forming in her eyes.

"Of course not...! You both are all I have and I love it here, but I have been assigned to set up our branch in Paris... it's only for about a year and after that, I have a surprise for you all."

"What...?" Devi and Ranjit shouted in unison.

"I will tell you after I am back. Anyway, this time I am here for a week before I leave. I wanted to spend some time with you guys."

"Make sure you come back alone. I want an Indian daughter-in-law, not anyone foreign," Devi warned her son jokingly, but the message loud and clear.

"Now, I will not even have someone to talk to; as it is it's only once a month that you visit... a year is a long time," Ranjit told his son.

"Papa, all your relatives are here, you are highly qualified. Why don't you do something for the village? It's what you always talk about—to actually work for the people. Now is your chance," he said respectfully.

"That's what I have been telling him, but he hasn't even left the building since we came here. In fact, a villager had come asking—" Dilip's phone rang, and he excused himself and went to the balcony.

"Don't complain about me to my own son. Show some respect," Ranjit told his wife.

To give them space, Devi left. The father and son talked for hours, both of them extra careful not to tread on each other's toes this time.

"So... setting up an office in Paris, huh? Lovely city, romance in the air... a city just for the romantic," Ranjit pulled his son's legs.

"Maybe, but I am sure I will be so busy setting up the office that I will not have any time for the romance in the air. I did not know you had been there."

"Yeah, a long time ago, I had been sent for a month's training before you were born, an all paid vacation on public money," Ranjit said, taking a sip of the Jonny Walker, his son's gift.

Both of them occasionally indulged in a drink or two in the evenings. Ranjit never drank outside his house, a habit he had cultivated till date. It was the month of November, and the air was pleasant in the evening, perfect to sit down with a drink and relax.

The week passed in the blink of an eye. It was enjoyed by the whole family, especially the lady of the house, who was extra happy since her husband had taken a break from breathing down her neck for a few days.

Dilip left the next morning. "Papa, just think about what I said about helping the villagers," was the last thing he said as he waved to his parents from the window of his Toyota. Ranjit thought about what his son had said as he walked up the stairs.

"You know, this retirement has made me lose my bearings; never thought it would come so fast in my life. It just feels like yesterday when I joined the service," Ranjit reminiscenced, his wife hearing him out.

"I know, I remember your first posting and your resolve in wanting to do something for your country. You never gave up despite the hurdles. We were... we are very proud of you."

Ranjit thought for a while and said, "I think it's time for me to meet the old fellow. What was his name...? Dalluram?"

Dalluram sat in the living room, waiting for a cue from Ranjit to start. As soon as Ranjit looked at him with complete attention, he said, "Sahib, some company is planning to put up a power plant in our village. Most of us don't want to sell our land; we have been living on these lands for generations. What else can we do?" Dalluram stammered his concerns to Ranjit.

Ranjit thought for some time. "I will help you, but I can't do it alone. We have to be in this together. Can you organize a meeting of the village Panchayat with me?"

"The Panchayat already wants to meet you... anytime you want it. The representative of the company also wants to meet you... in fact, he is waiting outside right now. I saw him when I came in," Dalluram replied, relieved at the success of his mission.

Ranjit was surprised, "Why should the fellow want to meet me? Anyway, let's see. Call him in."

A shady looking man entered. "Sir, I am Reddy. I am in charge of land acquisition for the power plant," the man said, closing the door and tiptoeing towards the sofa.

"What power plant? We don't need any power plant. It will destroy our village and it will destroy the livelihood of the villagers. I have seen it happen again and again," Ranjit said with a sharpness that surprised even him. Reddy looked confused, suddenly being at the receiving end of his casual remark.

"What is wrong with you people? It's always only about profit. What about the people, their culture, their livelihood, their lives?" Ranjit continued lambasting him.

Devi watched with delight, the shades of her old husband returning.

"What livelihood? The fields hardly earn enough to feed them. The project will bring in development and employment. It will change the look of the village," Reddy said, trying to keep his cool. Ranjit got up in fury; the old bomb was ticking.

"Mr. Reddy, why don't you come tomorrow and let Ranjit sleep over it," Devi said, attempting to defuse the bomb. Reddy got up and went out without saying a word.

Ranjit looked agitated, the look of an old warrior, battle scars and all washed over his face.

*****

Reddy came back the next day, a bit more respectful, "Good afternoon, sir, how are we today?"

"Come, Mr. Reddy, sit down and let's cut the crap and get down to business without wasting our time," Ranjit replied, putting on his glasses.

"Sir, I wanted to meet you because you are educated and you know the villagers and you can make the villagers understand the benefits of the project, but yesterday…" Reddy got down to business, putting on the face of a seasoned negotiator.

Ranjit had dealt with hundreds of such people every day of his long career; he had eaten such people for breakfast, lunch, and dinner. This was exactly what he had been missing since the day he retired. He sharpened his claws and continued.

"Yeah, I am well aware of the big companies. They always have the people uppermost in their mind; it's never for profits."

"You don't understand, sir. Our company could have invested elsewhere, but we chose your village. Our management wants development here."

"No, you don't understand, Mr. Reddy. Just bringing in projects is not development. We don't want a power plant on our land; we would rather keep our land and generate income from it. The villagers have been doing that for generations and are quite happy about it, and it has proved to be a sustainable model. They are their own masters now, and once the land is gone from their hands, the money will vanish in seconds and then they will be working as your servants in the future. The only ones to actually profit will be your big company. They are simple people who are contented with their lives, so I advise you not to be a devil's advocate, Mr. Reddy."

"But sir, I can assure you that many villagers are more than happy to give us their land. I have already negotiated... ah... talked to them."

"Like I told you, they are but simple folks. Don't worry; I will talk them out of it." Ranjit gave a wry smile. "Have I made myself clear, Mr. Reddy? I think the meeting between us is over."

"You are making a big mistake, sir. We are going to put up a plant whether you like it or not. Good day, sir," Reddy took his leave, his threat lingering on.

Ranjit contemplated for a long time, confused about his next step.

"Why are you thinking so much? Half the villagers are your relatives. Go meet them, talk to them. In fact, this is the right chance for you to renew your bond with your people. Maybe even I can join you, I too can talk with the women," Devi told her husband, happy to be a part of her husband's worldly thoughts for a change. Previously, there was a strict unspoken law between them—no interference in official matters.

There was a knock on the door, and Dalluram walked in, carrying a basket of potatoes. He handed it to Devi without a word.

"You don't need to get us anything. We are one of you, and this is not an office," Devi said, carrying the basket towards the kitchen.

Dalluram just smiled and said, "Sahib, the Panchayat would like to meet you tomorrow. They will come here."

"No need, we will go to the village ourselves. I want to meet everybody," Ranjit replied to a grinning Dalluram.

***

The village was a typical village, just about in the process of being corrupted by development. There were about a hundred houses scattered all around. A rough lane divided the village into two unequal halves. A National highway passed from its outskirts, on the other side of which you could see rising buildings and some activities. Their apartment building lay across the highway like a giant observing them. The village housed a Temple and a Church indicating the faiths it followed. It had a small but functional health centre and a few alternative medicine specialists functioning from their shacks. A small market could be seen which grew in activity every Sunday, on the market day, or before any festival.

The duo of husband and wife walked into the village and were greeted by the villagers, who were gradually growing in numbers. They all wanted to meet the boy who had made it big. No one had made it so big from their village—an officer in the capital, who had visited numerous foreign lands and knew it all. It was like the return of the prodigal son.

Ranjit was as surprised by the reception as was his wife. At last, he felt a deep connection with his roots. He suddenly bent down and touched the feet of the elders who put their hands on his head and then hugged him. The hubbub increased with everybody wanting to talk to him all at once. However, there were some people who kept their distance, Ranjit observed.

The village elders, Panchayat, and the couple sat down on a raised platform of the village courtyard. The other villagers sat around, making a circle. The circle too was divided unequivocally. The undercurrent could not be seen, but it could be felt like a cold breeze flowing through the gathering, seeming even more prominent in the gathering, where everybody knew each other.

Mr. Reddy was sitting with the smaller group, and a smile cropped up on his face whenever their eyes met. The smile a fox gives to a hen. Ranjit smiled back, the smile of a hen who knows what the fox is up to.

The meeting commenced with the pros and cons of the project, pros headed by Reddy and cons headed by

Ranjit. As is the nature of such meetings, it concluded with no concrete outcome. Ranjit had fought a good battle with invigorated energy and surprisingly he felt happy, he felt wanted. A group of villagers surrounded him as they looked up to him for their salvation.

***

There was a knock at the door. Ranjit was writing on his pad, drawing up the battle plans, in the living room.

"Good morning, Sir," Reddy said with a slight bow.

"Mr. Reddy, it's no use trying to influence me," said Ranjit, making a gesture for Reddy to sit.

"Sir, I have once again come to request you. I have seen how the villagers look up to you. Please think about the good the project will do—the development, the employment. On top of that, we have planned a lot of social work as well."

"Mr. Reddy, like I told you before, I have seen many such projects. They benefit everyone except the very people who sacrifice their land, their livelihood, and their way of life. So you are not going to get any help from me. In fact, from tomorrow we are going on a hunger strike until the project is scrapped. Be sure that even if we lose, I will make sure the project is delayed beyond its feasibility. I have seen the effect of such projects first-hand, so please don't take me to be a gullible villager," Ranjit told him coldly.

As Reddy left, Ranjit told his wife, "You know this is what I have actually wanted to do my whole life—work for the people with the people, and not sitting far away from them in an office. This is my true calling."

The next day, the villagers went on a hunger strike, and Ranjit was catapulted from a retired bureaucrat into a leader. As Ranjit got weaker, the news went out and slowly reporters started pouring in. Ranjit had gone national, and the hierarchy of the people trying to convince him kept rising. Ranjit was ultimately taken to the hospital and had to break his fast, but he had already done the damage and the investors of the project slowly started having cold feet. Finally, the battle was over as the company decided to invest elsewhere.

The company withdrew from the village with its tail between its legs. Only Reddy remained to tie up loose ends and close their office. The day Ranjit was discharged from the hospital, there was a huge crowd waiting for him. He gave a brief speech promising to work even harder for the villagers and for the many rights that were due to them. The sleeping tiger had woken up again. Ranjit's life had again become full, he felt happy, he had finally found his mojo, and to Devi's delight, the nagging husband had retreated, hopefully never to resurface again.

***

The flight from Paris was delayed by an hour. Ranjit and Devi had gone to receive their son at the International airport in the capital. "Let's go and have a cup of tea, no use just standing here," Ranjit pulled his wife playfully, happy that their son would be back after nearly a year's time. He wanted to tell his son so many things, especially about his advice to help the villagers and the work that he was doing.

Some people at the airport even recognised him and came up to chat with him. "Ranjit, the IAS turned philanthropist," was how the media had branded him. The flight finally landed, and the pair eagerly waited to get the first glimpse of their son.

"There, there, I can see Dilip," Devi shouted in excitement. Dilip waved at them and walked towards them.

"He looks sad..." Devi said worriedly, her motherly instincts nagging her.

"No, he must be tired after such a long flight," Ranjit reassured her.

"Hi, Ma... Pa," Dilip bowed down to touch their feet.

"How are you guys? It's so good to be back," Dilip hugged them both, taking his time and enjoying the moment to the fullest.

"Oh, we are absolutely fine. I have so much to tell you, but first about you. How was your stint in Paris?" Ranjit asked his son, helping him push the trolley.

"It was great. I successfully set up the office in record time," Dilip answered proudly.

"You look sad... what's the matter?" Devi asked her son, ignoring the glare from her husband.

"Oh, it's nothing. Do you both remember the surprise I said I would give you when I was back? Well, it did not work out," Dilip said, crestfallen.

"What did not work out?" Devi asked, halting her walk to look at her son.

"You know, I had managed to convince the board to invest in a power plant in our village. I would head it eventually, and at the same time, I could spend more time with you guys. In fact, I would have been housed in the village itself... but some old fool instigated the villagers against it, and now my credibility is on the line."

Dilip's mobile rang. "Excuse me I got to take this call... Yeah! Reddy, you fool, what the hell have you been up to?" Dilip shouted on the phone as his parents stood speechless.

THE WATCH

The night lamp reflected an eerie red halo, giving the room a bloody complexion. The watch rested on Anjali's bedside table. On the steel strap was etched "Omega" like a proud man with his chest puffed up. Her father had gifted the watch to her. An imitation no doubt, but a good one, enabling the likes of her to flaunt it around people who mattered. It had earned her many compliments, and she always wore the watch with such panache that it dispelled all doubts in people's minds about its being a fake. She never went anywhere without the watch.

Today, she was in a hurry. She had to go to Siliguri for a meeting, alone. Siliguri was the nearest tier-2 city from Gangtok, some hundred kilometres away.

It was not the first time that she was travelling alone. People thronged there every day to shop, to catch a train or even a plane. Since childhood, she had always heard about the dangers of this big, bad city. She had heard several stories about how the plainsmen duped the innocent hill people. It had been hammered again and again into her head so much so that every time she crossed the inter-state border, her senses heightened, and she was on alert, perpetually ready to pounce on anyone or anything trying to attack her.

One could say she was being paranoid about leaving the safety of her home state, but the people of this small, peaceful state would scoff at you and elaborate on the many imminent dangers that lay beyond their safe borders, especially for an unescorted lady.

It was nearly seven in the morning, and the town was just about waking up from its slumber; shops had started to pull up their shutters. You could easily find shops open even at six in the morning. People here slept early and arose even earlier.

She hurried down to the bus depot, dragging a large bag behind her, the wheels emitting a long growl amplified by occasional pebbles and potholes on the road. The bag held the odds and ends for the overnight stay along with the regulation toothbrush, nightdress, and a book. She never went anywhere without a book, be it any book.

The bus was about to leave. She had no problems getting a ticket to Siliguri as these days most favoured the 'jeeps' that plied between the two destinations every half an hour or so. She preferred the safety of the government bus with the huge "Sikkim Nationalised Transport" emblazoned on its sides. Not that nationalised truly lived up to its grandiose name, as in reality the buses never ventured beyond the borders of Siliguri.

The journey from Gangtok to Siliguri is a relatively straightforward one, just follow the lone highway NH-10 for about hundred kilometres or so and you are at your destination. The roads are tortuous and winding; the black tar topping is almost always in patches, the major portion being eroded by omnipresent incessant downpours; and to add to that, the regular landslides ensure a bumpy and treacherous ride with the ever-persistent threat of a rock fall that can decimate you on the spot. Yes, the ride is dangerous and thrilling; combined with the scenic beauty of the valley and the flow of the Teesta alongside, it furnishes serene thoughts of dying with a smile. Once the hilly roads are over, the plains welcome you warmly, and, as you leave the hills, you leave the dizziness of the drive, the landslides, and the simplicity behind.

As the bus reached the plains and lumbered through the straight, smooth Sevoke Road, the fatigue of the journey overwhelmed her, and she started to doze off, her head rolling to one side. The bus stopped with a sudden jolt, rudely yanking her out of her slumber. She disembarked from the bus as the big digital clock on the station building announced the time to be 11:25 a.m. She had another three hours to kill before the meeting.

She dumped her solitary bag in the room of the hotel that stood a few meters away from the station. The building was old, but she always stayed here, as it was safe. A person from Darjeeling ran it, a hill-man. She walked towards a *rickshaw* and haggled with the *rickshaw-wala*, its driver, for a reasonable fare to the main market. She took a deep breath, the warnings of her well-wishers still ringing in her head; she clutched her handbag tightly, put on a stern look, and sat down on the antiquated transport.

She had no particular shopping to do, and so she roamed around aimlessly, walking and surveying the many shops around at leisure. The heat felt good, defrosting her stiff body, and slowly massaging her frozen innards bringing them alive after the cruel winter in the hills, the prolonged cold that slowly froze every muscle in your body like rigor mortis.

Suddenly, she collided with a woman—a chic woman with huge sunglasses and very high heels. "Shit... sorry," muttered the woman, shook her hand, and strutted off nonchalantly. Anjali was now feeling hot and decided to do away with her jacket. She carefully folded the jacket, laid it over her forearm, and continued walking. After about a quarter of an hour or so, she took the jacket draped on her right arm in her left hand and flicked the wrist around to check the time.

The watch was missing... gone. She screamed at the top of her voice, "Someone stole my watch!" Some of the bystanders stared at her in surprise. Panic engulfed her, and a medley of emotions began clobbering her heart. She stood still, her mind and body transfixed, trying to process the information in her brain and waiting for it to relay instructions. Suddenly, a bolt of realization struck her—she visualised the chic lady, the woman who had bumped into her and shook her hand.

Anjali retraced her steps and walked towards the direction the woman had taken. The woman could not possibly be far away, so she picked up the pace. The Hill Cart Road, crammed with shops on both sides, was the shopping centre of the city. Her eyes scanned the surroundings, trying to find the perpetrator. She slowed her pace as she peered into every shop for the flashy woman. She remembered that the woman had worn a bright blood red poncho, so it should be easy to spot her.

As Anjali headed towards the last stretch of the street, she suddenly saw the woman on the other side of the street. She had to cross the road to reach her. The cars came to a screeching halt as she crossed the street pell-mell, her eyes pinned on the woman, unaware of the pandemonium she was causing on the main road. She picked up speed and started running towards the woman who was unaware of the approaching bundle of fury behind her.

Her hands clutched the woman's shoulder tightly, compelling her to turn around swiftly. The woman looked at Anjali, her eyes a mix of shock and curiosity. Anjali took a moment to catch her breath, her hand still clutching a fistful of the woman's attire. The woman slowly removed her hands and stood still, her full attention towards Anjali, asking a thousand questions without uttering a word.

"You have my watch," Anjali said, the words coming out in gasps as she tried to control her ragged breathing. Patches of perspiration gleamed on her face.

"I beg your pardon?" the woman replied, a perplexed look on her face.

"I said you have my watch. Please give it back."

"What the hell are you talking about?" the woman countered with an irate look.

"Please give me my watch. It's very dear to me." Anjali raised her voice.

"What the hell are you talking about, and who the hell are you? I have never seen you before," the woman said looking at Anjali and then at the few bystanders who had gathered around to see what the commotion was all about.

"You have never seen me? Bullshit. You stole my watch," she screamed loudly, attracting more amused people to the already growing crowd.

"What the f*#k are you talking about? Shit! I have never been more embarrassed in my life. This bitch is crazy," the woman said, shouting back, turning red in the face.

"Hey, lady, you cannot just go around accusing anyone without proof. What proof do you have that this lady has stolen your watch?" someone from the crowd queried.

"Some time ago, this woman bumped into me and shook my hand and after that, my watch went missing. She is a thief... it is a gift from my father who is no more. It's very dear to me. Please help me... let her show us what is inside her bag," she pleaded, hot tears streaming down her cheeks.

"What the hell...? I am not going to show anyone what's inside my bag just because you say so. You can't just go around accusing people and checking their bags. I refuse to be treated like this by this idiot of a bitch," the woman screamed loudly in response and clutched her bag tightly towards her bosom.

"If you are innocent then just show me what is inside your bag, and if my watch is not there, I will just go," she offered.

"I don't care a shit whether you will go or not. I refuse to be blamed like this by anyone. I have never been so mortified in my entire life," the lady reiterated, trying to create a path through the crowd.

"I am not going to be duped by anyone. Do you think I am a fool just because I am from the hills? I am not going to let you go until you give me back my watch. I know your type—dressing up hep and stealing from people," Anjali said, gripping the woman's bag and pulling it forcefully towards herself.

"Madam, this is not going to solve the problem. It is better to solve it between yourselves before it becomes a police matter. Okay, let me be of help. Madam, you tell us the brand of your watch, and Madam, you check your bag yourself," one of the bystanders, a young man in his early thirties suggested, looking at both the ladies.

"But..." the woman faltered.

"Omega," Anjali said loudly for everyone to hear.

"What?" the woman uttered, turning white.

"Madam, do you have an Omega watch inside your bag?" the man asked, pointing at the lady's bag.

"Yeah, I have an Omega watch in my bag. I had given it for repair, and that is what I had come to collect. But it's mine, and I refuse to be treated like this by anyone."

"Okay, Madam, it's up to you as we cannot force anyone, but the police have to be called," the man replied.

"Just show me your bag," Anjali said, suddenly snatching the woman's bag forcefully.

The woman, taken by surprise, pushed Anjali, losing her balance and spilled the contents of the bag on the pavement. An Omega watch lay beside a lipstick on the ground. It was her watch... the same model.

"See, I told you that this bitch is a thief. It's my watch, and I am taking it," she said to the crowd. She picked up the watch and started hurriedly walking off before the woman could react. She was late for the meeting, and so she ran and got into a taxi. She did not see the lady running behind the taxi, hurling obscenities at her. She felt shaken; she took deep breaths trying to compose herself, wiping her face with both hands, the tears leaving invisible patches on her cheeks. The only good thing she felt was that she had been able to take care of herself.

After the incident, she did not feel like staying back in Siliguri. It had left a very bad taste in her mouth. She lovingly checked the time on her watch, the watch looking perfect on her wrist like an extension of her body. It was nearing seven. She could still get a jeep to take her back home. She hurriedly rushed to the hotel, collected her bag, and checked out. She was just in time to get a seat on the last jeep back.

It was past midnight when she reached Gangtok. The jeep stopped at Deorali, just a few minutes' walk from her home. She was nursing a terrible headache, the effect of a tiresome day and an even more tiresome journey back. It takes a toll on your body when you have to travel the hill roads twice, going down and coming up the same day.

She lived alone; she entered her bedroom and turned on the lights. She stood for a long time, her face ashen, and then she switched off the lights, put the night lamp on, slowly unclasped the watch, kept it on the bedside table, and went to sleep without changing her clothes.

The night lamp reflected an eerie red halo, giving the room a bloody complexion. The watches rested on Anjali's bedside table. On their steel straps were etched "Omega" like proud men with their chests puffed up.

LOVE AND AMBITION

The wind was howling and the rain formed a continuous chain of droplets up towards the sky as if the gods had opened millions of taps all at once. The trees swayed, dancing in the wind, stretching their limits. Lightning flashed, exposing a small house under the cover of darkness. Thunder followed immediately, trying to scare it away.

A man walked towards the house, escorting a woman, the umbrella somewhat reversed, collecting rain. The path was slippery, mud and water forming a paste that forced the two of them to hold each other for balance. The house looked nervous against the thunder and wind. The cry emitting from inside appeared like the cry of the house against the weather gods. The two finally reached the door, drenched, the umbrella laid in despair, crying aloud with an apology.

The house itself had only two rooms, if they could be called that—a bedroom and a room that acted as an amalgamation of kitchen, living and a second bedroom. The roof was thatched and the walls were made of mud and clay, having openings imitating windows. Plastic sheets hung over the openings that acted as protection against both wind and water and at the same time let the brightness in. The bedroom itself had one cot crafted from bamboo and a tin box that accommodated the belongings of the family. The kitchen had a kerosene stove and a long bench made out of bamboo.

The house had a single bulb, which hung from the joist of the door to the bedroom, conveniently positioned to light up both the rooms with a single flick of a switch. There were nails placed all around the house where you could see clothes hanging, removing the want of a closet of any kind. The main door was made from a tin drum that used to contain oil but was now flattened to meet up the requirements of a door. The toilet was a small shack outside the main block where one could just about squat. It had an Indian pot and a plastic container for water. There was a small field in which a few vegetables and patches of flowers grew. A path led from the main road to the house, a path created by repeated footfalls of the occupants.

The three male members huddled together in the kitchen in silence. The midwife closed the curtains of the bedroom. Sunita's cry escaped through the thin barrier, the cries increasing in strength until they became continuous. "Push harder... harder... harder!" shouted the midwife over the sound of rain and thunder. Finally, the wailing of a baby was heard as the cries of the mother subsided. The electricity went off, throwing complete darkness all around except for the lightning that repeatedly broke the darkness for a split of a second. A lantern was hurriedly lit, which returned some lost brightness. The lantern made from a bottle and a piece of cloth fluttered against the wind that entered through the various cracks of the rickety house.

Ravi, the third child of Vikram and Sunita, was born on that stormy night in a small village in the hills. His first cry was in tempo with the slow dripping of water from the roof of his home, dropping at regular intervals like dancing to a tune and announcing poverty to the world, rhythmically. Ravi wailed for some time before peace again reigned in the house, occasionally interrupted by thunder and wind. "A boy..." shouted the midwife for everyone to hear, the shout proud, as if she was responsible for the sex of the child, a male child.

Once the midwife had washed and cleaned the new-born, she handed him over to his father—a tired looking man with two thin gawky teenage boys, all staring nonchalantly at one more mouth to feed. Vikram was silently happy that it was at least a boy, as raising a daughter this side of the world was not very easy, especially so if you were poor and already approaching the wee hours of your life.

Sunita, lying on the cot, looked worn out after the strain her body had just experienced. There were still traces of blood and fluids on the sheets that gave off the stench of birth. Even though it was the third birth, each experience had been different and exhausting, if not more.

"The baby has to be fed and kept warm. The mother needs to be monitored for some time," said the midwife, facing Vikram almost accusingly as if this was entirely his fault alone. No one uttered a word for some time, silently trying to cover up the reason for Ravi being born after so much of a gap. When Sunita had announced her pregnancy, Vikram had felt a knife go through his heart like he had been conspired against. Sunita had undergone the 'procedure' at a government hospital, had she not? The doctor had been careless enough to bring another life into this world. Of course, the value of life in this part of the world is much less as compared to the west, maybe because there is so much of it. For Sunita, it was as if she had come alive again and at last, had some purpose in life.

The midwife handed the baby wrapped in a soft cloth to Sunita as the thunder roared in the distance. Sunita looked at her baby with a tenderness that only a mother can feel. The baby refused to suckle as if irate that it had been forced out of its comfortable environment and did not like it one bit. Sunita laid the baby beside her to try again after some time, encircling an arm around it protectively.

"We have to prepare soup for mother," said Vikram, signalling his sons to get ready. Ganesh immediately started the fire and put on a pan with some water. Buddha started to chop some cabbage with no idea whatsoever of where this was heading.

Escorting the midwife outside with the formalities completed, Vikram thanked her, "We are very grateful to you for the smooth delivery."

"I hope this will be the last one. You know at this age it's dangerous for both mother and child," she replied.

Vikram smiled sheepishly. "I know. It's not going to happen again. Tomorrow itself I will visit the hospital, but thanks again." With that, he turned and started to trudge towards the house, his head hung low more out of fatigue than shame. The storm had passed and the electricity was restored.

Vikram got down to creating space for the latest member of the family. It was like watching a magician at work, a pull here and a push there and lo and behold, some more space in the cramped house. Of course, everybody tried to ignore the loss of their share of the area, every inch as precious as gold. The baby's cot had been put up beside the mother's bed.

"I will repair the leak in the roof tomorrow and both of you better help me," Vikram told his elder boys, the tone carrying a hint of warning for them to be present at the said hour. The boys nodded their heads in the cosy knowledge of an empty threat.

The roof had been planned to be repaired every day since the start of the monsoons, which everybody conveniently forgot when the rain stopped. Once again, when it rained, they would wait for it to stop before any kind of repair could be undertaken and again the empty promises. A vicious cycle of threats and promises left the roof unrepaired day after day. Once the leakage got beyond their comfort, the roof would be ultimately repaired, come rain or sun.

The nights to follow would be full of wailing and errands that reminded Vikram of the early days of the birth of his elder sons. He did not like it at all, as his job demanded huge physical energy from him, sweat draining his energy drop by drop in the afternoon sun. Being deprived of sleep meant an already tired body before a hard day's work. He wished there was a woman in the house to take the responsibility of these feminine errands. The two boys were scared to even hold the baby as if it was a ticking bomb, no threats worked, but to be fair they did help in other ways.

Sunita too wished that she had a maid or even a daughter whom she could rely on. The male members could only carry out orders without any compassion, like a machine, an irritated machine. She missed her mother the most; she missed the pampering she was used to. She had secretly prayed for a daughter this time.

Sunita had not always been poor and had seen life on the other side. Her father had been in the army, and even though he could not afford time for them, he had comfortably managed to fulfil the worldly needs of his family. He used to visit them twice a year whenever his leave got sanctioned. She, at that time, had thought that the attention of her father was more important to her than anything else in the world. She now realized how wrong she had been. Love alone doesn't make the world go around.

It was attention that had attracted her to Vikram who had come to work in her garden when her regular *mali*—gardener—had been taken ill. Vikram, along with tending the flowers, had tended to her and taken her away to a world, which at that age looked to be full of adventure and promises. She had just passed her high school. Since then her conservative family regarded her to be dead and totally cut her off. She used to hope that one day her parents would call her or visit her themselves, or at least send a message. That day never came, and over the years, her tears had dried off crying for her lost family. She had tried a few times to talk to her mother, but her mother refused to have anything to do with her. Her father had told her candidly that she was no longer his daughter and was not welcome to his house. She had nowhere to go and resigned herself to the life she had chosen unwittingly. She hated poverty and inwardly never forgave Vikram but did not have the means or courage to show it. She too in her heart had pronounced herself as dead.

As for Vikram, like his father and his father before him, he knew no other life. Over the years his spirit had taken a repeated beating and had been sculpted into a perfect poor man, a man with no say, no choices. Life was tough and he had no expectations from life. All he wanted was to survive. He now did odd jobs as a labourer or *mali* whenever he could get a job, as their small field was not enough to feed so many mouths. He knew that he had deluded his wife and that she was not happy with him. Even though she tried to hide it from him, her eyes told him everything. But he did not have the luxury of keeping his family happy as all he could do was to keep them alive. Dignity, romance, and love are luxuries that can only be courted by the rich and are not intended for the poor. He too had dreams when he was growing up, but the dreams had slowly faded like the setting of the sun, only, never to rise again. His father and his grandfather had been labourers who migrated from their homeland for a better life. *Is this a better life?* Vikram had wondered many times.

From the time of birth, Ravi had around him an air of authority as if he was oblivious of his roots. This piqued his father and brothers, his father because it scared him and his brothers because it made them jealous. Nevertheless, it amused his mother who thought that if God has created him like this, then maybe he had plans for him. Being born into a poor family, only the God Almighty could make plans for the future, as they had neither the money nor the right to do so. It is simply a matter of day-to-day survival.

Poverty is a great tranquillizer; it takes away a man's voice, thoughts, rights, feelings, dreams and most of all, his dignity.

***

Over the years, Ravi turned out to be the blue-eyed boy of his mother, much to the chagrin of his brothers.

"Ravi, come fast, I have made some momos for you." This love-filled beckoning by Sunita had become routine in the house now. Somehow, he always seemed to get the best helping or an extra piece as if the gods themselves were on his side. He too acted like it was his birth right, which led to him being secretly scorned by his brothers. Sunita was so protective of her youngest that at times it felt almost as if she was as obsessed with it as the rich are of their gold.

"Ravi, I have bought a new pair of slippers for you. Try them on," Sunita shouted one day as Ravi came running happily. Sunita had used the money for her own prescribed medicines to buy slippers for her son instead.

"Now there is no money left for your medicine," Vikram said angrily.

"I don't need the medicines, I am fine."

"You are spoiling the boy; it's not good for him."

"He needed new slippers," Sunita replied as a matter of fact.

"So do Ganesh and Buddha, your other sons."

Sunita ignored his remarks and helped Ravi put on his new slippers.

Vikram watched with growing consternation but did not have the heart to tell her. He knew that somehow the world would ultimately confine the fortitude of his son. In this world, generally, only the rich got richer and the poor only got poorer.

"Next year I will start teaching Ravi the ways of our trade. He can join me for work. Maybe, unlike me, he can even become a head *mali* someday," Vikram announced.

This announcement made Sunita flinch with agony. That was the highest level her husband could dream about, as if being a gardener was a great thing. "Why a *mali*, why not something better?" she rebuked her surprised husband.

He let the rebuke go, blaming it on the postpartum blues. However, in his heart, he knew that his dreams were no match for his wife's dreams, the dreams he had snatched away with the promises of love. But, to plant dreams in your child without any chance of their being fulfilled, was downright cruel.

Ravi was eventually expected to help his father earn a living as both Ganesh and Buddha soon landed labourers' jobs in a faraway land and had to leave home with the hope of living in this world like their ancestors, nothing more, nothing less. They lacked the education that sometimes ignited dreams and gave hope, so they simply had to continue the legacy of the past generations.

Ganesh had come home one evening, announcing, "The Hydro Power Company needs labourers for their project in Himachal. We have given our names."

Vikram had nodded his approval even before Ganesh could complete his sentence.

"We will have to leave in a week's time."

Ganesh and Buddha were excited to be working in a faraway place, looking forward to any chance that life may bestow upon them. They were bored with just breaking stones for the road and were young enough to look for more challenges in greener pastures, hopefully.

Sunita had known that this day had to come as it had come many years ago in her husband's life. He too had left his family behind to go to greener pastures while his youngest brother had stayed behind to look after his parents. When the time came for her two sons to leave, Sunita could only cry within. She knew they had no choice as with a new kid it was getting difficult for them to manage.

"Please take care of yourselves, and don't forget that we will always be waiting for you," was all she could tell her sons. It was as if the world was cutting a part of her and taking it away. She had already bid farewell to one family; to bid farewell to her sons would be more difficult than before. She hugged both of them tightly, not knowing when she would be able to see them again. The boys were carefree but had turned out to be good and hardworking.

"Bye ma, we will be keeping in touch. Don't worry about us," both the boys said in unison and walked away before the tears started flowing down their mother's eyes.

Vikram acted tougher, put his arms around his sons, and led them away to the bus stand. "A man has to do what he has to do," was his only worldly advice to his sons who waved at him as they boarded the bus to their destination. Vikram watched the bus leave with his sons. There were others from the village— about eighteen boys in all were going, and that was at least some security. He had heard that often there were casualties in the construction of Hydro Power projects. He silently prayed that his boys be kept safe.

The departure of the two boys ushered in the next phase of life for them. The house again became spacious; two adult male members do leave a huge vacuum. Sunita's focus now totally rested on Ravi. Maybe the knowledge that Ravi would be her last caused her to be especially bedazzled by her youngest. She loved him more than life itself, as simple as that.

For Vikram it was life, as usual, work or else die. He had lost two pairs of helping hands but gained two fewer mouths to feed. All in all, the balance was once again restored—status quo. They got the news that the boys had reached safely and had settled down fairly well. "Tell Baba that we have reached and started our job. We are happy," was what Ganesh had told the postmaster Kishore over the phone. The postmaster had personally delivered the news over a cup of tea.

There had never been any question of Ravi ever going to school, and the topic was avoided like a taboo in their household. But Ravi did not understand poverty and always turned to his mother whenever he saw other children going to school in their uniform. "Ma, where are they going? I too want to go with them," he said almost ritualistically every day. Sunita's heart wrenched every time her youngest uttered those words.

"They are going to school. Maybe one day..." she used to reply, eyes brimming with tears, knowing that she was lying. She knew what her youngest son was missing, unlike Vikram.

"Promise...?" Ravi would look into her eyes and ask, fully confident that his mother would never lie to him.

You could almost see the growing resolve in Sunita's eyes.

Every Sunday, Sunita would take her youngest to the small market of the village. She would buy some sweets for Ravi, and then the two of them would walk back gleefully. On their way, they had to cross the orphanage. She would often see a smart woman standing outside the orphanage, staring at them and returning a smile when she stared back. One day, the woman, Mrs. Sen, approached them, introduced herself, and started talking.

"What a lovely boy. Does he go to school?" she asked inquiringly.

"We can't afford it," Sunita replied.

"Well... why not? There are scholarships and other means. You could try," Mrs. Sen enlightened her.

"Actually, Ravi wants to go. I have always wanted my kids to study, but my two elder sons could not go as they had to work for us to be able to meet our ends. My husband will kill us even if I talk about it," Sunita replied, taking out all her pent up feelings before this stranger who seemed to understand her ordeal.

"You know education is the only insurance against poverty. If you don't educate him, he too will never be able to educate his children and the cycle will continue. It's never too late; at least you can send Ravi," Mrs. Sen said as she waved them farewell.

"Meet me again; maybe I can be of some help," Mrs. Sen shouted as the duo was walking off.

Sunita and Ravi both stood for some time, contemplating the words of the stranger. A seed had been planted in their heads, a seed which could turn their world topsy-turvy.

As Ravi turned six, Sunita was determined that her youngest should go to school. She was ready to take on anyone who thought otherwise. That became the sole purpose of her life, and she was ready to do anything to accomplish it. She tried on many occasions to broach the subject with her husband but could not garner enough nerve to do so. Eventually, one day, she braced herself and spoke with Vikram.

"Ravi should go to school like the other kids of the village," she said in a timid voice.

"You are being shown big dreams by that Mrs. Sen," he said. "I have seen you talking with her. Just remember that we are not well off like her," shouted Vikram to a defiant Sunita who in this matter suddenly seemed to have developed the courage that had been missing over the years.

"You never listen to me; it's always your way. Ravi is different; he needs to go to school," Sunita insisted yet again.

Vikram tried but could not fathom how Ravi was different. "You think I don't want to send him to school? But tell me—how? I can hardly feed him," Vikram said, trying to convince his wife.

"I don't know how, but Ravi has to go to school," Sunita stubbornly argued. Vikram kept his silence, knowing this debate would lead them nowhere.

One day, as Vikram came home after the day's work, Sunita offered him a glass of tea. Then, she said timidly, "We have to convert to Christianity," as if she did not want anyone else to hear her words.

"Have you lost your mind, woman? What the hell is wrong with you? Why in God's name do you want to convert?" asked Vikram, perplexed.

"We have to convert to Christianity; we have no choice," said Sunita again in a zombie-like stupor, looking down and ignoring Vikram's reply.

Vikram threw his glass on the floor and got up. "Don't ever say that again, do you understand? We have been devout Hindus for generations and that's how we will remain," he said, really losing his cool this time.

"But Mrs. Sen..." said Sunita, but before she could complete her sentence, Vikram for the first time punched her in the nose and walked away, leaving the cowering Sunita and her bloody nose to themselves. Vikram felt like a coward, he had never laid a finger on his wife before. She had made him feel less of a man, not strong enough to stand up for his family. He did love his wife; he hated himself.

***

Ravi, now eight, was the first from his clan to see the inside of a school. Mrs. Sen somehow miraculously had him admitted—that too with a scholarship—into the public school in which she taught. Vikram was not very happy about it and every day regretted the day he had succumbed to Sunita's stubbornness. But now, the bullet was out of the gun for good.

He had tried to explain to his wife, he had threatened her and had even raised his hand, but nothing worked in front of his wife's rigidity in this matter. It was as if the devil himself had taken over her. Ultimately, Vikram surrendered and paved way for Sunita's tenacity. For Sunita, nothing mattered as long as her son was going to school and refused to talk about it to anybody who queried. The only blotch in her otherwise perfectly executed plan was that Ravi would, from now on, be living in a hostel and would be home only during holidays. She missed her youngest.

"It's for his better future... It's for his own future, and I can visit him in school," she muttered, more to convince herself than anyone else.

***

The school was very big and housed within a campus of about hundred acres. It was a world within a world. It had three wings—primary, where Ravi was at present, junior, and senior. It had a rich tradition of more than one hundred and fifty years and was built by the British for the British. It was much later that Indians could study there but within the ambit of the traditions left behind by them.

The buildings itself were majestic stone structures, embedded with centuries of history. If you closed your eyes, you could actually see its history and feel the English loitering around. There were numerous sports fields, tennis and basketball courts, and among others, an Eton Fives court, truly making this school one of its kind and among the very best of the country.

Mrs. Sen had Ravi admitted through the faculty quota and sponsored him herself, disguising it to look like a scholarship to his parents. If they knew that she had sponsored him, maybe they would have refused. The poor sometimes have much more self-respect than the rich do in mundane matters.

The first time Ravi entered the school campus, he gripped Mrs. Sen's hand tighter and felt his heart beat faster.

"Don't worry, Ravi, you are really going to like it out here, and I am around whenever you want anything," said Mrs. Sen, smiling at him.

Ravi looked around like it was a dream. The school was so big, not like the one in their village. There were boys staring at him. They were dressed very smartly and looked every part of the environment. Ravi felt scared but tried to put up a brave front.

"Is this the school where I will be studying?" Ravi asked, still quite unsure. "It looks so big."

"Don't worry. I am sure in a few days you will adjust perfectly and be happy," Mrs. Sen assured him.

Out of his environment, Ravi looked very unsure, like a fish out of water. He stuck to the side of Mrs. Sen as they walked into the Principal's office.

"So, this is the boy," the Principal Mr. Thomas said, looking at him caringly. "Welcome, Ravi. I hope you will like it here with us," he said, giving Ravi a big smile in an attempt to make him comfortable. Ravi did not utter a word.

"Well, since he has had no formal schooling, we will have to put him under special care until he catches up. I am sure he will be able to cope," the Principal said to Mrs. Sen.

"Oh! He is a bright kid. I myself have been tutoring him for a few months now. He will easily cope up," Mrs. Sen said, taking leave.

"Best of luck, Ravi, I will be talking with you later," the Principal said, going back to the paperwork he was doing.

"Come, I will take you to your dormitory. It's the room which you will be sharing with your friends." Mrs. Sen pulled Ravi towards a building.

Mrs. Sen showed him his bed in the dormitory; he had always slept on the floor in his house. "It's time for me to go. You better start getting unpacked," Mrs. Sen said, showing him his locker. Ravi caught her arm; he did not yet want her to leave.

"Boys, help your new friend Ravi," Mrs. Sen called a group of boys.

"Hey Anil, help Ravi here. He is going to be in your class," Mrs. Sen said as she left the dormitory.

The first time they had met, Anil had called him a dumbo and had got a punch on his nose as a reply. Ravi was definitely much tougher than the boys at school were; life had made him tougher. Anil had mumbled a hasty, "Sorry, can... can we be friends?" and stretched his hands towards Ravi, who had delightfully taken it. With the punch, Ravi had struck his first friendship in the school. Anil helped him unpack and taught him the intricacies of the system. Trunk, linen room, locker, dressing gown were all new terms he was exposed to as he unpacked. Anil introduced him to all the boys, "This is Ravi, and he can punch like hell."

There were general greetings welcoming Ravi. Sometimes a punch is much stronger than words or riches, especially in the world of small boys who are yet to be sophisticated by the ways of this world.

The dormitory accommodated about twenty boys with ten beds each on either side alternating with a tall locker. Ravi sat on his allotted bed, surrounded by the boys all talking together, nearly as excited as Ravi. It was suppertime, and Ravi was escorted down to the dining hall, a hall that accommodated about three hundred boys.

"You know the food is very good here, nearly as good as my mother's," Anil told the awestricken Ravi. "Do you like Indian or Continental? We get both," he continued his orientation.

"I... I like both... What is Continental?" Ravi asked a surprised Anil, who forgave him his ignorance.

"Oh, don't worry. You will see for yourself."

The food, whatever it was, was the best he had ever eaten. You could take any amount, without feeling guilty. At home, he would have to think before he went for a second helping; otherwise, sometimes his mother would have to sleep on an empty stomach. Here, he was amazed by the variety and the fact that no one gave it one bit of importance. He put everything that was there on his plate and started eating, the food more important to him than the numerous amused eyes focussed on him.

After supper, the boys had 'prep time,' short for preparation time. Ravi was shown his desk in his classroom, and the duty teacher handed him his books. After 'prep' it was bedtime, and a tired Ravi changed hurriedly into his night suit, minus his underpants—a rule of the house—and jumped into the inviting bed. His body felt tired due to the long journey, and his mind felt tired due to a new world. A slight frown betrayed the anxiety that he felt in this strange place away from home. A smile slowly formed on his lips, a product of his dream and this welcoming, friendly, and safe world.

Ravi was awakened by a rude clang-clang sound, sleep still clinging on to his body. He got up thinking for a second that he was sleeping on the floor of his house. He shook away the sleep and tried to orient himself to the new surroundings. The boys had already started their morning ablutions; he was yet to understand the routine and the ways.

Anil, as usual, guided him, "Get ready, we have to go for Chota Hazari and then P.T." The words again confused Ravi, 'Chota Hazari... P.T...' He just followed the rituals the boys undertook. Chota Hazari turned out to be a cup of milk and some biscuits and P.T. was basically exercise.

That was followed by a visit to the Chapel, then classes until lunch and then sports and hobbies. The cycle continued except for the holidays when they were free almost the whole day except for a little bit of prep in the evenings followed usually by a movie show. The thing that amazed him the most was the 'sunshine holidays,' a surprise holiday whenever a bright sun adorned the sky. This was a luxury as being located in the higher Himalayas the sun god hardly visited them. This was a day meant for them to bask in the sun, laze around, and dry their damp clothes and beddings.

"Hey, Anil, let's go to Blackies," Ravi shouted across the football field.

Blackies was the school canteen that used to be run by the Indians during the British Raj, hence the name, Blackies. His journey in this very different world had started. It was a totally altered journey, where he could think outside the world created by his parents or bound by poverty. He started taking small faltering steps into this fantasy world.

The education cleansed him both physically and mentally. It was like a gradual cleansing of the dirt of ignorance and poverty from his body, leaving a diminishing trail behind him that eventually faded.

Ravi slowly started integrating into his new world, to which his old one gave way. He made many friends who were all from the world of money. In school, the uniformity hid his poverty, especially with a little help from Mrs. Sen whenever necessary. This was a fantasy come true for Ravi, and he was willing to do anything to stay on here. Initially, he was put in a special class, but he worked hard and soon started bridging the gap like a premature baby trying extra hard to survive. The boys gradually accepted him as one of them, and it helped a lot that Ravi was very frank and down to earth, a rarity in such an institution.

Just after a few months in school, his life until then seemed like a bad dream, shunted to his distant memory only to rudely recur whenever the thought of his parents crossed his mind.

As time passed, he loved the school and he loved Mrs. Sen who was slowly turning out to be his godmother and slowly replacing Sunita in his heart. The boys too thought that Ravi was her relative. He made friends with boys who would not even give him a second look if he was still in his village. There were games he had not even heard about and a whole world waiting to be explored by him. He dreaded the day his past would catch up with him. He wanted to erase his past, especially before his newfound friends discovered it. He dreaded the day his parents would come visiting him. He had recurring nightmares of them visiting and the boys finding out about him and giving him a tough time.

He told Mrs. Sen about it, but she said, "Don't worry. I will take care of them. You just concentrate on your books." There was a slight twinkle in her eyes.

***

Sunita lived for this visit. She put on her best attire and made Vikram do the same as they readied for a five-hour bus journey to the school. Vikram felt very backward and small and was more apprehensive than happy about this visit.

"He must be really missing us. I hope we reach in time," she said happily, looking forward to seeing her youngest after a gap of six months. It had been a long time since Vikram had seen his wife happy.

On the bus, she told anyone willing to listen, "We are going to visit my son; you see he is studying in a boarding school." The other passengers thought that she was crazy and maybe they were going to visit a psychiatric. Their clothes reeked of poverty, and the box that contained *Halwa* even more so. Sunita had woken up early in the morning to make *Halwa*, which was Ravi's favourite dish, and packed it in a tin box that she held close to her bosom. She was sure he would love it. The bumpy ride did not dampen her jovial mood as she was living her life through her youngest.

"I am so lucky," she told Vikram, conveniently forgetting to include him in her world of happiness.

Sunita and Vikram walked through the school compound looking at each other, unsure of how to behave. The two looked every bit a misfit against the pristine and imperial backdrop. Their unsure movements magnified a thousand times by their conscious minds, they slowly shuffled through the field and reached the quadrangle. Sunita beamed with happiness when she saw her son. He looked so smart, so handsome, like any other rich kid. Her chest swelled with pride, and her eyes had tears of joy. She did not even care about the other children staring at them.

Vikram did, and was happy that someone he knew was approaching them. "Good afternoon, Mrs. Sen," he said poking his wife to get her attention.

"How are you? See, he does not look like your Ravi anymore. Did you recognise him?" Mrs. Sen said, smiling.

"I will always recognise my son, no matter what," replied Sunita sharply, slightly hurt by Mrs. Sen's words.

"That's not what I meant; I mean look how happy he is. He has been doing wonderfully in the school and has been really progressing well. Don't get me wrong, but I think you should not visit him anymore in the school. He will anyway be home at the end of every year during the holidays," said Mrs. Sen, looking at their faces for any kind of emotions.

Sunita and Vikram kept quiet at Mrs. Sen words.

"The other kids don't understand, and it will be hard for your own Ravi. If you want him to touch the sky, you will have to let him fly," she said.

Sunita managed to hold back the urge to hug her son, to kiss him, to feed him. Unwitting tears welled her eyes, which she quickly wiped turning the other side.

Sunita was quiet during the whole journey back home. "It's for his own good, it's for his good future," was all that she could whisper to herself repeatedly, hugging the unopened box of *Halwa*. "Now I have to wait a year to meet my youngest," Sunita said to her husband as they reached back home, her face twisted with agony.

For Vikram, it was not a question of a year, but that they were not good enough to visit the school of their son. Sunita could not and did not notice the subtle changes in her son. Vikram was aware of this slow metamorphosis, and it scared him. He had seen the look of shame on his son's face. He had wanted to run away from the school, leaving his son at peace. He dreaded the future, which would be totally out of his hand. He had been seasoned enough to expect only the worst from life and was scared of his wife's growing expectations, and his son's growing ambitions.

He was willing to make the sacrifice. But would his wife be able to face the future?

On the other side, when his parents visited, Ravi saw his mother and father standing nervously in the quadrangle, the centre of the school surrounded by buildings all around. Ravi was confused, and at the same time was ashamed of them, but he could not understand why. How could the hate for what his parents represented be more than the love he felt for them? He was ashamed that his friends would see his parents. He wanted this feeling to pass as soon as possible and counted the seconds until it was time for them to leave.

As his parents turned to leave, he started missing them; he wanted to go with them. He, a kid, could not understand the two very different worlds that he had to hop between. It was only a matter of time and logic before he would have to choose between the two.

***

The year was over and it was time for the holidays which lasted for two months. All of Ravi's friends got ready to leave; Mrs. Sen and he would be among the last to leave.

"Where will you be during the holidays?" enquired his friends.

"Sikkim," he replied. Mrs. Sen would drop him home as she always visited the orphanage in his village and stayed there during the holidays.

"I don't have anyone to report to," she told Ravi as they drove towards the village in her car.

"Where are you from, Mrs. Sen?" asked Ravi, feeling happy for the holidays. He had worked very hard and badly needed a break. Now that he was going home, he missed his mother. Here, he did not need to hide his poverty and was not ashamed of her. He was but a boy still confused about his emotions.

"From Kolkata... have you heard about it?" she said, changing the gear as they approached a climb.

"Yeah, in Geography class. I would love to visit someday," he said, putting on his coat, as it was getting chilly.

"Maybe one day you will. Let's see."

"You know, I have not thanked you for all that you have done for me. You changed my life," he said as they entered the village.

"You are all I have," she said as she drove away dropping Ravi near his house.

Sunita had been waiting for this day for a year. She saw a boy walk towards the house with a black bag slung across his shoulder. He looked smart and had the shine of wealth; it was as if he was in the wrong place, standing out like the sun in the sky. As Ravi approached, she stood transfixed, overcome by emotions, silent tears just flowing like an undammed river. Ravi ran up to her and hugged her. He had become nearly as tall as his mother.

Vikram stood at a distance, looking at his son with a sigh of relief as he saw him hug his mother. He walked towards his son and held him tightly; he did not want to let him go again.

"Pa, you are crushing me. How are you both? Really missed you both," he said with an accent making them both smile with pride.

Sunita had been secretly saving a little here and a little there for quite some time now. She had laid out a spread to celebrate his homecoming.

"How are Ganesh and Buddha Da?" Ravi asked, taking a mouthful of chicken, the juice of which escaped and dripped down his chin.

"They are fine, but we have not heard from them for a couple of months. They did send some money last time," replied Sunita, joining in on the feast. Vikram too was enjoying the feast and his son, who in just an year seemed much more sophisticated than anyone he ever knew.

As days passed, everyone he knew in the village started to look up to him. Even Vikram proudly started to count on his advice. 'Ask Ravi' was his regular repartee.

Initially, Ravi did enjoy his homecoming and his parents, but the novelty started wearing off with each passing day. He again started noticing the poverty that he had really started detesting. Everything out here reminded him of his poorness. He started to miss school and the talks of his parents started sounding petty and small. He missed his friends, food, sports, and everything else. He started to hate going to sleep on the floor again or having to squat in the small unhygienic toilet. He even started to despise the ways of his parents, which felt so backward.

To keep his sanity, he started visiting Mrs. Sen in the orphanage and began volunteering. His parents were proud of the work he was putting in. He had no friends in the village and did not want to make any. Whenever neighbouring boys came to call him, he always had an excuse ready. Sunita refused to accept that her son was not happy at home. Vikram felt his fears slowly taking shape as he watched his son over the days.

Soon enough, two months passed, and it was time for Ravi to go back to school. Mrs. Sen came to pick him up. Sunita smiled at her with a grim face, trying to hide her sorrow.

"Don't worry, Sunita, I am there with him. He is turning out to be a wonderful kid. See how much he helped in the orphanage," she said as she held Sunita's hand tenderly. Ravi stood still, looking at his parents and trying to comprehend his confusion. He was going to miss them no doubt, but he wanted to be away from them, he missed school more.

"Don't worry, Ma, the year is going to pass so fast that I will be back before you know it."

Sunita stifled her tears and took her son in her arms before letting him get into the car. Vikram carried his bags and delicately put them in the boot. He came around and kissed his son on the cheek, an emotion that he had never shown before. Vikram and Sunita bade their son farewell and stood motionless until the car disappeared around the corner. Then they slowly went inside, neither uttering a word, thoroughly drained by their emotions. A year is a long time, and time stretches and becomes longer if you wait for it to pass. Sunita had already started to wait for her son's return as soon as his steps left the house.

As the car slowly moved out of the village, Mrs. Sen could see that Ravi was upset, though he tried to be brave.

"So, how were your holidays?" she asked, trying to liven up the atmosphere.

"I do miss them, you know—it's just that I am so confused. I hate their lives," he said, looking for some kind of reassurance from her.

"It's okay, everybody gets confused, and it's just that you are trying to adjust to a new environment. Don't think about it too much, and everything will work out. It always does," she replied, smiling as he smiled back.

For some time, all was quiet as the car gained altitude and the village below started to shrink in size.

"Tell me about yourself. I don't know anything about your family," Ravi asked lazily as he snuggled into the comfortable seat.

"There is not much to tell. I think you should sleep... it's a long journey back," she replied softly as the road started descending towards the river. Ravi dozed off, his head swaying in tandem with the curves in the road. Ravi's question had brought back distant memories and a dreary feeling in her heart.

"Tell me about yourself" was a simple enough question. Sometimes a simple question raised many other questions, requiring complex answers that one may not have. What was she doing here? Why had she run away, leaving her friends and family behind? What was she running away from? She looked back in time, trying to remember her previous life.

Her parents used to call her Pam, short for Pamela. She lived in a big mansion on the outskirts of the city, which had a huge compound. Her father was a well-respected businessman owning numerous hotels. Her mother was a sweet woman who had followed her passion for teaching. Pam, their only child, was the leading light of the house. Her parents loved her, and in spite of leading a busy life always found time for their only child. She loved the compound of their house and spent many happy days playing around in it.

As she grew up, she found out that she too shared the passion for teaching like her mother—passion passed down from mother to daughter and the capability to understand each other perfectly. Overall, she had a perfect life which one shade less or a shade more would not have been the same.

They reached the designated spot for lunch—a small motel standing precariously over the riverside. "Ravi, wake up—it's lunchtime," she shouted, shaking him out of his deep slumber.

Ravi was hungry. "We are already halfway there?" he questioned, his mouth already watering as the smell of cooking whiffed in the air.

"First wash your hands; have you forgotten your hygiene? What would you like? I will be ordering," she said as she washed her hands and took a table for them.

"I love *momos*; we don't get them in school. Two plates, please," Ravi said, taking a chair opposite her after washing his hand hurriedly.

She did not feel hungry, but they would be reaching late and there were no stops in between. "I think I will have *rotis*," she said loud enough for the woman standing at the counter to hear.

They ate quietly, one was hungry and the other was not. Both had lots of thoughts weighing in their minds. They hurriedly finished lunch and got back in the car.

As they continued the journey, dusk approached. "How can you sleep through the whole journey, you lazy head?" Mrs. Sen cried at Ravi who was again looking drowsy.

"It's the food; let's put on some music," Ravi said, flicking the radio on. *'Take me home to the place I belong... mountain Mama take me home...'* the radio roared, pushing Ravi further deep into a trance and Mrs. Sen into her memories.

Salim... her love Salim. He too had a passion—like her—for teaching and genuinely thought that that was where actual nation-building started, teaching and moulding young minds for a better nation. The first time they had met was at the school. Sometimes, in life, you meet someone with whom you involuntarily connect as if continuing from where you had left before in the realm of time, in the cycle of life. That was Salim and Pam, united by time but separated by religion.

They joined in body and soul and followed the same passion, creating their own small world full of happiness. But like in many instances in life, someone was bound to bring religion in between and so it happened. The loving Dad and Mom became strict disciplinarians, forbidding Pam to have anything to do with Salim. They rudely snatched her from her small world and put her under house arrest. No one knew about a storm brewing inside her stomach, until the day it started showing and caused a bigger storm in her home when she refused to abort.

The biggest storm was when her father gave her the news of the fatal accident of Salim—a lorry just outside the school gate had crushed him. Her world was brought to an untimely end, maybe to be continued in another realm, another cycle. She had no choice but to abort. She could still hear the words of the doctor clearly, "due to the complication of late abortion, Pam will never be able to conceive again."

The last storm brought her world crashing down. Her guilt-ridden mother told her about the truck that crushed her beloved Salim, "You see Papa had your best interest at heart." Devastated, Pam just left everything and headed for the hills.

She had a friend volunteering in the orphanage in Ravi's village, who welcomed her. She stayed there for about a year, completely immersing herself in the running of the orphanage. She worked so hard that the ghosts of her past slowly started distancing themselves from her. One day her friend said, "Why don't you apply in the school? I heard there is a vacancy and you are a certified teacher. You can visit us during the holidays."

She had been leading that life to date.

Until the day she saw a woman and her small cute son walking past her window. Something made her pay attention, as if looking for salvation. The boy, though poor, had in him the strut of a king. Chest out and head held high. Tiny but big, poor but confident, illiterate but wise. She did not know why she felt a stirring in her heart when she saw the boy. That was why she had befriended Sunita, Ravi's mother. The boy awoke in her the feeling that she was never destined to have again. But she could dream, couldn't she?

"Are we there yet?" Ravi asked, rubbing his eyes and forcing himself awake.

She had tears flowing down her cheeks, which she hurriedly wiped clean. "Yeah, it's about time. I am tired too," she whimpered, driving through the huge gate and taking the turn towards the hostel.

Ravi too was tired and headed straight for his bed. Most of the boys were back and already asleep. Ravi thought about his parents, especially his mother, and missed them. He knew that after some days his parents and home would take their place in the distant memory. He had seen Mrs. Sen cry and wondered why she had not told him about herself. "I will ask her again," he thought before the car lag got to him, making his eyes droop and then close.

Ravi was back again in his dreamland and started the life which he really looked forward to. Slowly, he began making his mark in the big scheme of things. His secret was his desire to excel in everything supported by the unending zeal of energy that sometimes seemed unnatural to others.

Others had no reason to excel as their life was already mapped out for them, most of them following the footsteps of their dynasty. His life was an adventure where the path had to be made by him, so he worked hard. The routine of life carried on as the years flew by, and he slowly blossomed into a confident adolescent. The only hitch was that gradually a gap grew with his parents. Even during the holidays, the conversation became increasingly formal over time, as they were living in a totally different world and had nothing in common with him.

***

Ravi entered the sixth form, the final year of school. Mrs. Sen too would be retiring at the end of the year, and there were talks of her returning to Kolkata. She had finally made some peace with her parents when a few years ago her father suffered a major heart attack. That was the only time she had gone back home. Now her father had passed on, and everything had been handed down to her. Her ageing mother was running the business, proxy for Mrs. Sen, and had been begging her to come back. She wanted to complete her term in the school, which had given her refuge at the time of her need.

On the other hand, Ravi had not thought about his future. But now as his scholarship ended with school, he started to worry. He had talked with Mrs. Sen, but she had just said, "Don't worry, something will come up, you just concentrate on your final exams." He had not brought up the subject with his parents, as he knew they were helpless.

Ravi had made some solid friends for life bound by the years spent together; they swore by each other. The school authorities were somewhat lax in discipline towards the sixth formers, and the boys took full advantage of it. However, as they were the senior-most, they had the responsibility of setting an example for the juniors. They took it rather seriously as it was a form of self-discipline and would ready them to face the adult world.

The boys studied hard as the exams approached. Ravi wrote his final exams with a heavy heart, wondering what the future held for him. It was a tearful farewell for the boys, who promised to keep in touch throughout their lives. They were still innocent, protected by the school and unknown to the ways of the world. They did not know it yet, but the school had made them ready to face the world. Ravi's school days ended.

Mrs. Sen wanted to drop Ravi home and visit the orphanage for the last time before she left for Kolkata. The drive back was sombre as each thought of the unsure future ahead.

"Are you going back for good?" Ravi asked, his heart missing a beat.

"Yeah, I have to; I have been running away from life for a long time now. I have a mother, too, you know," Mrs. Sen replied, looking at the bright boy whom she had been grooming for a long time.

"I know nothing about you, about your life..." Ravi remarked, hoping for some revelations.

"Maybe one day, you and I can have a long chat. Life is full of surprises, you know," she said, smiling, "One thing I have learnt is that life is not worth running away from. You have to face it full on."

Ravi tried to take in the wisdom that Mrs. Sen had just handed to him, "Sometimes one may not have the opportunity, though," he said.

"I have told you before—don't worry too much. It usually works out in the end. If you have been able to come so far, maybe you are destined to go further... have a little faith," she said, taking the turn towards the village.

"How time flies... school finished so fast that I can't believe it. I am going to miss school," Ravi said, sadness creeping into his heart and tears forming.

"I know life is short, but we should forget the past and live in the present. Don't worry," she replied, this time taking the car right up to Ravi's house.

Sunita and Vikram were sitting outside the house, waiting for Ravi. They rose together as the car approached their house. Mrs. Sen made her way towards the house followed by Ravi, who carried a huge suitcase in one hand and a duffel bag in the other.

He had grown much taller than his father and looked every bit a gentleman. Sunita increased her pace towards him, smiling broadly and trying to help him with his baggage. Vikram stayed back, arranging the bamboo stool for Mrs. Sen.

As Mrs. Sen waited to talk with his parents, Ravi went to put his luggage inside. The luggage looked every bit out of scale against the size of the room. Sunita came inside to make tea and said to Ravi, "Mrs. Sen wants to discuss something with us. You go and join them; I will get some tea for everybody."

"So, have you thought about Ravi's future?" Mrs. Sen asked Vikram, who had a defeated look, "He has worked hard and is an excellent student. He deserves to study further; he deserves a better chance, a better future."

Vikram looked at Sunita, trying to understand what Mrs. Sen was implying. Sunita looked at her husband, words failing her.

"Let me be frank with you. I have no one and I will be more than happy to take Ravi with me. He can join a college in Kolkata and join me in my business after that," Mrs. Sen said, the words hitting Vikram like a sledgehammer. A worried look formed on his face as he tried to read the emotions of his wife.

"We have not thought about it," Vikram replied, not sure how to react but becoming more defensive.

Sunita finally spoke with a trembling voice, "I feel we should let Ravi decide. After all, it's his future."

Vikram had dreaded this day since the day Ravi had joined the school. He looked at Sunita and could see a look of deep despair. He looked at his son, who had a look of surprise on his face. He knew that the future being offered to his son was something they could not compete against, but he also knew Ravi was already not theirs. Their other sons may come back but never their youngest. Without implying anything, Mrs. Sen had claimed their son. In his heart, he knew Ravi was already gone.

"I will visit as often as I can," Ravi said, declaring his decision softly.

Sunita ran inside, tears streaming down her cheeks. Hearing what Ravi had just said felt like as if someone had pulled out her heart. She still remembered the day he was born; he was special to her. She remembered his small hand clutching her own on the way to the market. She remembered the way he used to look at her, with complete trust. She remembered the way he would look at her when his father reprimanded him. She remembered the look on his face when she had promised to send him to school. Every memory of her son suddenly came flooding back, making her sit down on the floor. Tears would not stop; they just kept on pouring. She would have gladly sacrificed her life for him.

She remembered the first time she had met Mrs. Sen. She remembered the day just after Vikram had punched her nose.

"Vikram will give his life but will never convert to Christianity, and the Father in the school nearby will never admit my son. I have no other option... Oh God, there has to be some other way," she had told Mrs. Sen, crying.

"There is a way, but..."

That was the day they had made the deal; that was the day when they both had got what they wanted. That was the day she had offered her love in order to give her son a better life.

For, there is no greater love than letting go...

THE NIGHTMARE

I woke up with a throbbing pain in my head and an urge to relieve myself. The room was pitch dark. I got down from the bed, my feet seeking the slippers that were usually beside the bed. Not there... must have left them somewhere else. I got up and moved towards the toilet door, only to come against a bare wall. What the hell? The doors moved... I moved ahead, feeling the wall with my hands scanning for the door. Ah, the door, finally... My head was really throbbing, and any second now, I would just let go right here. The door handles... the handles felt different. I turned the handle and then opened the door. It was dark and I could not see a thing—the electricity must be off again, I never switched off all the lights. Suddenly, stairs appeared out of nowhere, and I tumbled down. I reached the bottom of the stairs and then just let go, a warm liquid trickling down my legs... I passed out.

I came back to my senses, and this time my whole body throbbed with pain, the outcome of the fall from the stairs. I slowly got up, trying to catch my bearings. Dawn was breaking and a hazy brightness was entering the room, enabling me to see the silhouette of the house. It was not my house... Shock broke over me. 'Where am I? Have I been kidnapped, or am I still in my dreams?' I pinched myself, but nothing changed; the exact same silhouette remained but this time looking a bit eerier. Had I gone mad, or had I lost my memory? 'What is my name?' My name was Priyanka—that is all I remembered. I slowly got up to examine the surroundings. The house was big, bigger than I had ever seen... But what was I doing here? I slowly walked around, and the brightness got stronger. I could see the dining table and a kitchen further down. I lost track of time.

Suddenly, a door opened, and a lady walked out, wearing a silken gown with some sort of a nightdress underneath. "Priyanka you are up so early? Go back to bed. Today is Sunday. You usually sleep through breakfast," the lady said, not even batting an eyelid at the sight of her.

"But since you are already up, I want you down for breakfast. It's been a long time since we ate as a family," she continued, going back to where she came from.

Priyanka needed time to think, and so she rushed back to her... to the bedroom and locked herself in and sat on the bed. The room was nice and big and just above the bed was a huge picture in a golden frame. The picture was of her holding a camera and smiling. She did not remember the picture.

There was a knock on the door. She slowly got up and opened the door. A cute girl of twelve was standing outside, looking at her curiously.

"Priyanka Di, here is your tea. Breakfast is also ready, and you are wanted downstairs, immediately," the little girl said, handing the small tray to her. Then she turned and ran down.

Now, Priyanka was confused. How did the girl know her name? She had never seen the girl before... What has happened to her? She drank the tea, went into the bathroom, and took a long cold shower. Maybe that would clear her head. Wrapped in soft towels, she saw the wardrobe, opened it, and put on clothes, trying to find her sanity. She tried to think hard... nothing, she didn't know how she had come to this house... and the lady and the girl, she had never seen them before.

Priyanka slowly walked out of the room and went down the stairs, one at a time, buying time. There were three people chatting merrily at the breakfast table. A maid was busy shuttling between the table and the open kitchen. One spot was empty, the cutlery already set up, waiting for her presence. She went to the table and stood for some time behind the chair, which she was sure was meant for her. Everyone stared at her as she pulled the chair to sit down.

"Priyanka... what is wrong with you... you have been behaving strangely since morning," the woman said, looking at her and pushing the bowl of porridge towards her. 'Me...? I have been acting strange? What is wrong with her, acting as if I was her daughter or something?' Priyanka thought but just kept quiet and started eating. The food tasted delicious, and she did not know it but she was famished as if she had not eaten for days.

"So, baby what is your plan today? Maybe, you and I can sit down and have a chat. You look agitated," the man turned towards her with concern. She was still thinking and had not thought through her next course of action.

"No... Uh, I think I will rest today... not feeling too well," Priyanka said, still eating. 'Baby... the man called me baby.'

Priyanka suddenly got up, muttered a soft 'excuse me,' rushed upstairs to the room, and locked it. She did not come out the whole day. She sat on the bed trying to think, trying to put the facts in place.

'I should call someone, friends.... but where is my mobile?' Priyanka combed the room for her phone. It was not there. She checked her bag for the wallet that contained her cards... numerous cards, which would definitely confirm her identity and her address. She found it—her driving licence, debit card, and her UID. All of them read—Priyanka Chettri, d/o Kumar Chettri, House No. 302, Arithang, Gangtok. Now she knew her next course of action.

She refused dinner and stayed in her room, biding time. Slowly the sounds in the house started reducing until all was quiet. She looked at the clock hanging on the wall. 11:00 p.m. said the hands.

Now was the time.

She opened her door, tiptoed down the staircase, reached the foyer, and went for the door. It was locked and could not be opened from inside. She checked the windows. All had iron grills. The kidnappers had locked her inside; they had known that she would try to escape. She went to the kitchen, saw a narrow door, and opened it from inside. She was outside.

She was finally free. Now she would show them—she was a brave girl, after all. She saw a taxi parked outside. She ran and opened its door and slammed it loudly shut, shocking the driver out of his nap.

"What—who—where, Madam?" the driver muttered with an irate look.

"The police station, please," she said in a whisper.

"Which police station?" the driver asked with growing interest.

"The nearest one, of course," she replied.

The driver looked with curiosity in the rearview mirror before igniting the engine.

At the station, a young Inspector was on duty, probably just inducted. He looked tired and sleepy; a cup was on his table out of which he took small sips now and then. Priyanka walked up to him and started talking all at once in broken sentences, "I was kidnapped—I ran—not my house—you have to help—there are a woman and a man—a little girl."

The Inspector beckoned her to sit, smiled at her, and offered a glass of water. "Now Madam, just keep your cool, and we will slowly take it from the beginning. I am here to help you." He took out a pen and opened a pad. Priyanka sat down, drank the water, and kept quiet.

"Okay, tell me slowly. What's the problem?" he asked her.

"I have been kidnapped and kept locked in a house by a man, his wife, and his daughter. I managed to escape in a cab and came straight here," she said, breathing heavily.

"Don't worry, Madam. We will take care of it. Do you know the place?" he asked, writing on his pad.

"No, but I have kept the cab waiting outside. The driver knows."

"Good. Bhola, call the driver inside," he told a fat constable who was listening with boredom, sleep plastered on his face.

"Take Madam's and the driver's statement, and tell them to get the jeep ready," the Inspector instructed another constable.

***

The lights of two vehicles moving forward in tandem sliced the darkness as the police jeep followed the cab. Priyanka was lodged between the Inspector and the driver in the jeep with the four constables at the back.

The cab screeched to a halt outside the house, followed by the jeep. The Inspector ran to the door of the house and rang the doorbell. Slowly the lights started being turned on like a cascade, from up to down. The door opened, and a man in a gown answered with a somewhat irritated 'what,' his eyes widening at the sight of the police and turning into shock at seeing the girl.

"Baby... what is the meaning of this, and why are you outside?" he said, pulling Priyanka towards him.

"What is all this? Priyanka, what is wrong? How the hell are you outside? Please tell me what the hell is going on?" a lady joined the man, shouting at Priyanka.

"Let's all go inside—we will wake up the neighbours. I want some explanation from all of you," the Inspector declared.

Once they were inside, the Inspector continued, "Now, everybody listen carefully. I want you all to keep shut. I will be the only one doing the talking. You will only reply when told to."

"First, the facts—this young girl had lodged an FIR saying that the people of this house have kidnapped her. They have kept her forcefully in the house," the Inspector informed the gathering.

Silence could be heard loudly across the room.

Everyone stared at Priyanka. A girl of twelve walking into the room and broke the silence saying, "I heard noises. What is wrong; who are all these people?" The little girl directed her questions at the man and sat down beside him clutching his arms.

"Inspector, I am her father. What is all this nonsense about kidnapping?" the man said, looking at Priyanka.

"He is not my father," Priyanka replied with conviction.

"Shut your mouth, you bloody fool. He may not be your father, but if it was not for him, we would all be dead. How can you say such a thing after all that he has done for you? He has literally brought you up, and he loves you more than he loves his own daughter. Is that not enough for you? What about your real father—the bloody drunkard, has he even come once to meet you, does he even care whether we are alive or dead? And why all this all of a sudden? Has anything happened, has anyone told you anything?" the lady shouted at Priyanka and started crying.

The man got up and went to the lady saying, "It's all right, darling... I am sure she did not mean it that way."

"She... she is not my mother; I have never seen her in my entire life. I don't know what she is talking about," Priyanka screamed at the top of her voice.

The room once again went silent; the sharp gasp of the lady could be heard reverberating in the room.

The Inspector, looking more perplexed by the minute, decided to let the matter take its natural course. He said, "I think this is more of a family matter than anything else. But I have to investigate."

"No! You have to believe me. I have been kidnapped, and I don't know anyone of them... this is not even my house. See, this is my driving license... and that is my address," she said, handing over her cards. The Inspector inspected the cards and gave a look of concern.

"What is your name, sir?" the Inspector asked the man, looking at the cards in his hands.

"Kumar Chettri. I am an engineer... she is my daughter. Well, I married her mother after she was born but I brought her up and she has been calling me Papa since she was this big," he told the officer, taking his hand to the level of his knees.

"Bhola, check the address of this place right now... wake up a neighbour or two. Bloody shit!" The officer was losing his cool, "In the meantime, I sure would be grateful for a cup of tea," the officer requested, looking at the lady.

The constable returned after a while, his brow filled with droplets of sweats. "Sir, the address is correct, it's this house," said Constable Bhola, his bulging stomach proudly pointing towards a man standing at the entry who was looking as confused as the situation at hand.

"Who's the fellow?" The Inspector put up the question in the open, putting down the steaming cup on the table.

"Sir... the neighbour; I woke him up," Bhola announced his achievement.

"Sir, I am Professor Singh. I live in the house next door," the man introduced himself.

"Oh... good, please come here. We have a situation here. This young lady here claims that this gentleman kidnapped her. Do you know them?" he said, pointing out the man and Priyanka.

Professor Singh stood aghast, staring at Priyanka and the man by turns.

"Do you know them or not? It's a serious allegation," the Inspector repeated himself, feeling tired as it was nearing dawn and he wanted to wrap up the matter and go home to sleep.

"Yes, of course, I know them very well. I live next door. He is Kumar Chettri, and she is his daughter Priyanka. Come again, who kidnapped who...?" The Professor put back a question.

"All of them are lying. I am sure they are in it together. You have to believe me. I don't know any of them. I have never seen them in my life. I have been kidnapped... you have to believe me," Priyanka screamed.

"Madam, enough, please don't include us in your family feud. We have much more important things to do. Next time I will arrest you. Waste of time and waste of public money! Case closed," saying that the Inspector walked away, followed by his team.

"Bloody shit... what a night," the Inspector muttered as he left, "Why do I always get the loony ones?"

The situation in the room was like a volcano about to erupt. Everyone stared at Priyanka, the little girl started crying, and the woman put her arms around her and tried to pacify her. Kumar looked worried, and the Professor did not know whether he was supposed to be coming or going. Priyanka glared at the man but held her tongue.

"Baby, tell me what is the problem? You always tell me. You are my princess, aren't you?" Kumar asked Priyanka, trying to bring the situation under control. Priyanka kept her silence, the silence louder than any words.

"Priyanka, what is wrong with you? Come tell your Mama. You know we all love you," the lady said, crying. Priyanka just stood still with no reaction.

"Kumar, something is wrong with her. Please let's take her to a hospital," the lady said, pulling at her husband in frenzy.

"I am going to the room... I need to lie down," saying that Priyanka simply got up and walked off, leaving three faces staring at each other.

"Something is wrong... everyone can't be in this together, something is wrong with me. They sure don't behave like they have kidnapped me. Why can't I remember them... not even vaguely? Why can't I remember this house...?" Priyanka thought hard, trying to recollect her past. "My house... I can't remember anything. What about my family? Shit, I don't remember anything." A chill went up her spine; something sinister was at play... but what? The throbbing headache was returning with a vengeance, and she felt faint. "I should lie down for a while," she thought.

Kumar sat beside his sobbing wife, trying to pacify her. "Don't worry. Everything will be fine. We will take her to the doctor in the morning. Maybe she is not being able to cope up with her new job... don't worry."

Mala kept crying, and the little girl sitting beside her looked petrified. Mala got up and slowly walked up the stairs towards Priyanka's bedroom. She had been inside the room the whole day and Mala was worried. She tried to push the door open, but it was locked. She thought of knocking but waited for some time before she could bring herself to knock. The door remained closed; she knocked again, louder this time. After a while, the door was slowly opened.

Priyanka, dishevelled and speechless, stood in the doorway. Maya pushed the door and walked into the room with Priyanka following. "What is the meaning of this, Ma? Let me sleep. I am very tired and today is Sunday, isn't it? Let me sleep some more. Feels like I haven't slept the whole night... What time is it?" Priyanka said in a sleepy tone.

"It's nearly five in the evening, and you have been sleeping the whole day," Maya told her, trying to understand what was happening.

"What...? But I went to bed early last night at about nine. Ma, have you been crying?" Priyanka asked her stunned mother. Mala ushered her daughter down the stairs and into the living room where the rest of the family were parked.

"Hi, Papa... What is wrong? Ma is acting strange and looks like she has been crying. Hey Chotki.... you tell me," Priyanka stood, waiting for an explanation. Mala looked at Kumar, her eyes crying for help.

"How are you feeling, Priyanka? You remember anything about this morning?" Kumar asked, still confused at her seeming normalcy.

"Me...? I am fine, Pa. Why... what is wrong? Why is everybody acting as if you have just seen a ghost? Remember what?" Priyanka retorted.

"No, no, everything looks fine now. Let's forget about it. By the way, I have sent a week's leave to your office. I think you need a break," Kumar informed his daughter.

"Why... and without asking me? Anyway, good... I wanted some break, too. I feel tired. Why don't you all also take the week off? We can all go somewhere," Priyanka appealed, squeezing herself in between her father and her little sister Nandini. Nandini gave way grudgingly; the age gap between the two was more than a decade.

"So Chotki, where do you want to go?" Priyanka asked her sister teasingly.

"Don't call me Chotki. How many times have I told you that my name is Nandini," she answered back with a scowl.

"Chotki... Chotki... Chotkiiiiiii. You will always be Chotki to me," Priyanka continued her teasing.

"Stop it, the both of you. Sisters are supposed to love each other," Maya lambasted the two.

"Good idea... let's all take a break and take a vacation. Let's go to Goa; it's been a long time since we all had a break," Kumar announced to the delight of his family.

"Yess... Goa!" the three ladies shouted in chorus.

The family sat down for dinner, everyone tired due to the day's events. The situation had somewhat normalized, but some worry lingered on; it could be noticed in the way the couple looked at each other and at their eldest daughter. Priyanka seemed oblivious to the day's happenings; it was as if her memory had been wiped clean, as if it had never happened.

"Mama... What is wrong? You look worried and you were definitely crying that time. Papa, is something wrong?" Priyanka kept inquiring, keeping her spoon down and looking up at her parents.

"No, Baby, everything is fine now, and don't worry, your Mama is fine," Kumar assured her and gave her a big smile.

Priyanka loved her father, actually her stepfather. He had never let her feel that he was not her biological father; in fact, he was closer to her than to her younger sister. He was a soft man, and care and love were his natural ways. Her mother was a lucky woman; they were all lucky, after all that they had gone through. She still had vague memories of her actual father, she could still hear her mother's cries, and she could still see her drunken father thrash her mother. But all that was in the past, as they had a good man to look after them now, to love them.

"Girls, take your milk up to your rooms, and don't forget to drink it, especially you Nandini," Maya instructed her daughters.

"I will drink after some time; I have got some homework left, but I will get yours, Di," Nandini informed her mother and her sister.

"Thanks, Chotki, you are such a darling, I will be reading in my room for some time, not yet feeling sleepy," Priyanka replied, looking tenderly at her sister. The family slowly retired to their respective rooms one by one.

I woke up with a throbbing pain in my head and an urge to relieve myself. I put my hand forward, waiting to feel the bedside lamp. I could not find it. In the darkness, I again used my hand as a scanner, scanning for the door or light switch. I found the switch and pushed it on, flooding the room with brightness. I thought of nothing but the bathroom, the urgency of the need totally usurping my focus. I found the toilet door, ran to the commode, and urinated, enjoying the pleasure of relieving myself. As I got up and turned, I saw a young girl, slim and pretty, staring at me. I screamed... she screamed back.

What...? How did she enter? What was she doing in my toilet? Why did I not hear her come in? I was sure it was a ghost—she did seem very pale, ghastly. I shut my eyes out of fear and tried to compose myself, but I failed—my breathing erratic, my heart pounding beyond my control. I slowly opened my eyes, one at a time. I could see the ghost lady doing the same. Do ghosts also feel scared? The one in front of me seemed petrified. Seeing the ghost scared somewhat boosted my courage. I reluctantly put my finger forward to touch her, to check if she was real. The ghost too lifted her finger in synchrony with mine. I went forward gradually, and finally, our fingers met. It was hard, hard glass. I spread out my hand and felt the glassy surface; it was cold and hard. It was a full-length mirror and the ghost lady was me.

My head was really throbbing now, and my heart was pounding as if it wanted to come out of my chest. I felt faint and took the support of the cold walls. It was a mirror, it reflected my image... but I could not recognise myself. I took deep breaths, trying to get my brain working. My name is... my name is... what? Nothing came out of my head; it was as if it was blank. I tried to think... anything. Nothing, my head was as clean as a whistle. I sat down on the floor and started screaming, screaming till my lungs hurt.

Someone was trying to open the door... no, break open the door. My screaming continued; it just kept coming. Finally, the door burst open, and a man, a woman, and a girl came running towards me, shouting, "Priyanka... Priyanka... what's wrong?"

Priyanka was sitting on the floor of the bathroom, screaming. Kumar ran through the bedroom with Mala close behind. He took his daughter in his arms and hugged her tightly "Baby, it's ok... it's ok. Papa is here." Mala stood transfixed, staring at her daughter. Nandini started crying.

"What's wrong with her? Something is wrong with her," Mala started shouting to no one in particular.

"Shut up," Kumar shouted at Mala, trying to control her hysteria. The hug slowly eroded the scream but Priyanka went limp, the screams having sapped all her strength.

"Help me carry her to the bed," Kumar shouted at his wife. The two of them carried her to the bed and sat on either side of her. Mala and Nandini started to cry.

"Shut up, the two of you... control yourselves. We have to take her to the hospital," Kumar made his intention clear. Priyanka had lost her consciousness.

Kumar and Mala carried Priyanka and put her in the backseat of their 'Ford Ecosport,' a new car they had just bought on the insistence of their daughters. Mala too got in and cradled Priyanka's head in her lap. Kumar hurriedly got in the driver's seat, shouting "Nandini, look after the house... be sure to lock it from inside and call your grandma at once," saying that, he put on the emergency lights and zoomed off, it would be at least a half an hour's drive to the hospital.

Mala kept murmuring, "What's wrong with my baby?"

Halfway through the drive, Priyanka stirred, slowly opening her eyes. "Where am I...? Where are we going...? When did I get in the car?" Priyanka fired a series of questions.

"What happened, baby? You suddenly started screaming and then you fainted. We are taking you to the hospital," Kumar stopped the car and turned towards the back.

"When...? I don't remember anything. I took a glass of milk and while reading a book I fell asleep. That's all I remember... I don't remember anything after that," Priyanka replied, trying to think back.

"Are you feeling fine now?" Mala asked, somewhat relieved to have her daughter back.

"Anyway, we have to go to the hospital. We have to get you checked up. Don't worry, just a routine check-up," Kumar stated, turning around and starting the car amidst the protests from Priyanka, "I am fine, let's go back."

The sun was slowly rising over the horizon, and the sky took the look of a gradually brightening screen. The hospital was still quiet but for activities in front of the emergency signboard. Illness had no timing, giving true meaning to the word emergency.

They drove into the parking area and then slowly hiked towards the neon sign. After explaining the symptoms to the duty doctor who kept turning towards Priyanka after each sentence, the doctor checked all her vitals after which they were told to wait for Dr. M. Basnet, the psychiatrist, who would not be in for the next few hours. The trio went to the canteen for some tea and tit-bits but more to pass time than out of hunger.

***

Dr. M. Basnet listened attentively as Kumar explained the problems. 'Interesting case,' he kept repeating, indicating his bafflement. Priyanka matched the doctor's bafflement as she too heard her father talk.

"My God... I don't remember anything," she kept telling her mother. Mala looked more relaxed like she had handed over her problems to someone with a readymade solution.

"Let us do a few tests and a C.T. scan before coming to any kind of conclusion," Dr. Basnet said. The whole day was a series of tests and scans, running from one end of the hospital to the other and then the same routine of collecting the reports.

"Amazing... absolutely normal," Dr. Basnet said after analysing each report. "Nothing... Idiopathic," Dr. Basnet declared the diagnosis.

"What is it, Doctor, what is wrong with her?" Kumar asked after hearing the complex word.

"Well, it's very hard to say, but I think maybe she is under stress or maybe it is due to trauma in her childhood. The human brain is a complex creature. Physically she is absolutely fine, nothing to worry," Dr. Basnet told Kumar.

"I don't understand what exactly you are trying to say," Kumar told the doctor.

"Well, let us do one thing. Let's observe her for some time. In the meanwhile, I will prescribe an anti-anxiety medicine for her for a few days—that usually does the trick," the doctor recommended.

The three of them drove back in complete silence. It was already late evening when they reached the house. Nandini was eagerly waiting for them and was relieved to see them, especially to see her mother smiling.

"What is wrong with her?" Nandini asked.

"Nothing... just stress, new job," Kumar replied, sitting down heavily on the couch. Mala and Nandini went to the kitchen to prepare dinner, and Kumar and Priyanka stayed back on the couch.

"Priyanka, baby, just remember you can come to me whenever you have any problem. You do know that I love you," Kumar tenderly told his daughter.

"I love you too Papa," was the reply before the room again became silent.

After dinner, everyone went to their rooms. Nandini took a glass of milk to her sister's room and bid her goodnight. Priyanka drank the milk and took the pill prescribed by the doctor.

Nandini went to her room, took out a bottle from her pocket, and put it back in a box under her bed.

I loved my sister... that is until I came to know that she was really not my sister. She acted as if my father, my father... loved her more. Look at her cheek—always teasing me, calling me Chotki in front of everybody even after I told her not to do so. So what if she got a job in that lousy news channel? Papa and Mama treat her as if she is a princess. I am the princess, I am their real daughter—can't they, especially Papa, understand that? She gets all the new stuff, and I the real daughter, get all the hand me downs. I really hate her. Luckily, I told grandma about it. She hates her too. She is my grandma and not hers. I love grandma and she loves me—only me. The old man... Sadhu, at grandma's instruction, gave me the medicine to be put in her milk every night, and in ten days he promised that she would be mad and out of the house. He had said something about hallucination and dementia. It seems to be working. Now, only seven more days left. I am the princess... only me.

Nandini had a look of jealously and hatred in her eyes, not the jealously of grownups, but pure and simple, unadulterated jealously and hatred, the one where the consequence does not make sense and it does not matter. She had a smile on her face as she fell asleep, contented.

I woke up with a throbbing pain in my head and an urge to relieve myself...

BHUL – THE MISTAKE

It was almost day break. The festivities were long over, and saffron, white and green were scattered all around the place. Numerous flags still fluttered, refusing to end the occasion.

A woman in her early twenties, covered from head to toe, walked at a brisk pace, in a hurry, scanning the area to check the presence of any other mortal. If you looked carefully, you could see that she tightly clutched to her bosom a small bundle wrapped in a cloth. Occasionally, she wiped her eyes with the back of her hands.

She finally reached a bylane in between two buildings. She stood for a long time, unsure of what to do next. Suddenly she put the bundle down quickly, turned around, and briskly walked away. The wailing sound of a baby echoed in the air, the sound distinct in the silence of the night, cutting through the darkness.

The woman stiffened on hearing the wail of the baby and then increased her pace, leaving behind a hint of guilt lingering in the air, the guilt only noticed by the fluttering flags as daylight lazily crept over the distant horizon.

The 15th of August is a very important day, marking the independence of our country. It was the day I was thrust into this world, a very important day for me. Of course, it's a different story that on this very day my parents left me in the gutter to make my own way in this world. Why, you may ask? It's a question thousands of babies like me will ask again and again; given birth without our consent and left alone, left to fend for ourselves when we needed nurturing the most.

At least my parents had the sense—or in fact sense of humour—to place a note on me, announcing, 'Bhul—Born on 15th August 1975.' I could at least celebrate my birthday with a name on the cake, in panache. But I still can't understand why the name 'Bhul.'

Talking about names, you know how significant names are in our country. Of course, some names are much more important than others are. If you have the right name, it can get you the world—this country being fascinated by big names. In that context, I think my parents gave too insignificant a name to me, though it has a nice ring to it—'Bhul.' Maybe Rahul or Akhilesh would have been more appropriate and could have made my life a lot easier.

So, that was the way I came into this charming world. I am now a beggar by profession even though some may say, 'What? Begging a profession?' Let me guarantee you that begging is as much a profession as any other, if not more. I am going to explain how I came across this profession. Let me also tell you that I have been gifted with some extraordinary powers, which I have used on many an occasion... but I am getting ahead of myself.

Foremost, 1 will affirm to the world right now about the truth of my parents and the reason they had to leave me. First of all, let's get that out of the way.

My father's name was Vikramaditya and my mother's was Gayatri. Like his name suggests, he was from a very rich family—they ruled the land. Like her name suggests, she was from a poor family—her father was a priest. They had one day met in a temple and had fallen madly in love. One passionate night they created me out of their love. But like any other love story vis-à-vis Romeo and Juliet, Heer-Ranjah, and Soni-Mahawal, they could not be together forever and were separated by this cruel world. My mother secretly gave birth to me and left me in the gutter with only a cloth wrapped around me along with a note for company.

Oh, how my mother must have cried, how my father must have missed me...

So, that is the story of my parents. At least that is what I believe happened, that is what I hope happened. It's not easy to give birth to your own parents, you know. Parents are supposed to give birth to you and not vice versa; but of course, the birth of a child also heralds the birth of parents.

Now, as far as my religion is concerned, I follow faith accordingly to the approach of an upcoming festival. Sometimes I am a Hindu, sometimes a Muslim, sometimes Christian, and sometimes even a Sikh. I follow all religions and it's a must in my profession—imagine all the festivals and all the free food and happy charitable people. People give most when they are happy; they take when they are sad. So you see in life, firstly you have to be happy yourself before you can distribute it around. I have also learnt that happiness is a habit that has to be developed despite the numerous kicks that life gives you. You have to keep on practising it.

So, I had been left by my parents in a *gully*, a bylane in between a police station and a brothel. I was lucky that constable Singh wanted to answer nature's call early in the morning and had slipped outside in order to avoid the filthy *thana* toilet. He saw my note and me and handed me over to the orphanage. I had survived.

In a sense, you can say he was like a father who protected me. Maybe he was, he could be... anyone could be. That is the beauty of my life: all my options are open. I mean, can anyone change their parents or especially their annoying relatives as per their own convenience? I can.

Anyway, I have very fond memories of constable Singh. He would occasionally visit the orphanage and see how I was doing. I guess that since he discovered me, he had some responsibility towards me. That stopped after some years as he probably felt that I would manage on my own from then on. He was the one who told me about the note my parents left. I can still picture the constable, tall unlike me, dark, muscular, a patch over one eye and a heart of gold.

The orphanage itself was not very big and could accommodate about twenty of us in two dormitories, one for girls and one for boys. The two-storied structure had the dining area and the office below, and the nun's quarters and our rooms above. It was a building, just a building and nothing more to it. A building built with a stretched budget and functioning with the bare minimum facilities, like a cactus in the desert, to go a long way with little. An orphanage run by nuns with the meagre donations they could accumulate.

They did try to arrange some kind of education for us. Given that there were not enough resources, the nuns sometimes taught us, on and off. You learn a bit, you forget, and then you learn the same again. Like a pendulum within its own confines, to and fro, more of a formality than anything else. We too did not mind, as we never understood education.

It was a tightly run ship and any flouting of rules resulted in a sharp reprimand. The rules, however, kept changing as per the moods and whims of the management, and it confused us to our wit's end. One aspect, however, remained constant: we had to pray twice a day. We prayed in a small room called the 'store.' However, every Sunday, we were made to parade to the Church for the service. People would stare at us. We looked like a line of urchins undergoing punishment, but it was still fun being out of the orphanage.

Of course, when there is a collection of orphans who have been instilled discipline through fear and not love, sometimes it is bound to snap. The bond of love is much stronger than the bond of fear or so history has proved time and again. So, under the innocent façade, we did get up to many adventures of fun in the otherwise boring setting. The nuns may not call it an adventure, but everyone has the right to their own views. Praying may be fun for them but not for me—I guess it's different strokes for different people.

From the time I can remember, there would occasionally be a brilliant one whose idea of fun we all endorsed. I will tell you a few as I remember. Chronology does not make sense in an orphanage where all the days seem alike.

I remember the time I and two other boys stole a chicken—actually stole is a strong word as the chicken had entered our compound. Technically, no one can blame us and call us thieves. So, a chicken had wandered into our compound, unseen by anyone under the blanket of the night. It's not easy catching a chicken, especially the one that creates a ruckus while being chased, but what is a chicken as compared to three hungry orphan boys. It finally succumbed, though grudgingly.

Now, catching a chicken is fun enough, but there is no use of an uncooked one besides playing with its stupid beak. We had to have a fire, but to have a fire in the dead of night is a sure giveaway. So we made a fire inside our room and roasted the carcass until it turned ...roasted. It tasted good, but the aroma it left behind baffled the nuns out of their wits the following morning. The whole orphanage effused the aroma of the delicious roast. The innocent look on everyone's face did not help one bit, but the evidence had been digested overnight and deposited in the single washroom one by one. The nuns could only keep their silence due to the lack of evidence. Of course, we removed all traces of the fire and the rejects.

To be fair the nuns did try their best to keep us happy; only their idea of fun was a bit different. Sometimes they treated us with a movie. A white screen was set up in the courtyard, and we all sat down cross-legged on the floor with the nuns in the background on their chairs. It was fun, even though we could hardly understand those movies—Moses, Ben Hur, Christ, and so on. The one movie I thoroughly enjoyed was 'Sound of Music' and I found myself humming the song for days—'Doe, a deer, a female deer...'

Then, of course, there were the occasional picnics, once in a blue moon to be fair. Some great soul during Christmas every year would sponsor a picnic for us. That was fun, and this time there would really be good food. We would wake up early in the morning and get ready. A bus would come to our gate, and most of us—barring the few newborns—would board the bus and sing happily all along the way. This time the nuns too would join in our festivity. They took us to different spots every year, and the day would be full of fun and frolic. We did have some fun in the orphanage, and most importantly, they kept us safe.

Nothing bad happened to me in the orphanage, but nothing good happened either. Occasionally, couples who could not conceive would visit the orphanage with the intention of adopting one of us. The nuns would announce this the day before. When the potential parents came to select a child, I would take a morning bath, not forgetting to wash behind my ears, put on my best attire—if it could be called that—select a spot which would be most visible, and try to put on an adorable look, as adorable as I could look.

No one adopted me even when I tried to look and behave my best. As if that was not bad enough, one of my friends would be chosen. Not only would I not be adopted, I would lose a friend too. The funny thing was that the couple would check out the children as if they were shopping in a mall, and we would all humour them, hoping against hope to be the one. Life always kicks you more than once and not necessarily always in the butt.

Nobody ever wanted me; in fact, I would myself have not wanted me. You see, I had been born with a somewhat blemished façade: one eye blind, white—where the pupil should have been, a cleft lip and a nose that seemed to point in the wrong direction. The more adorable I tried to look, the more people were in for a shock. Some of the women—and even men—have let out an audible gasp at the sight of me. And when they realized that I was not, in fact, a goblin, they tried to cover up their embarrassment by hurriedly handing me some sweets or money. Thus, in short, no one adopted me. In fact, from birth itself, maybe anyone could see that I was wasting my time and that my true calling was begging. I was perfectly designed for it like a bird is for flying or a woman is for a child.

For some time you don't miss anything and anyone; you are just happy with what you get, eat, play and sleep... that is all life is about. Then the brain starts growing faster than your body, creating thoughts and wants. You start to understand your surroundings and realize what you don't have. It destroys your bliss and makes your dreams bigger and bigger until you realize that it's too big for your boots, that it's too late.

You try to act brave along with the group who have been dealt the same cards by the dealer. You turn the card, surreptitiously hoping to read 'adopted,' but mine always read 'rejected.' You carry on year after year, brave, until your companions become smaller and smaller in age. Then you start to panic. Hope still lingers in your heart, hope which refuses to go away like a chewing gum stuck in your shoes, but finally, it has to die like everything else.

I was nearly eighteen and fully illiterate when I finally gave up the hope of being adopted and having a foster family. Even the godly nuns sometimes conveyed unintentionally that I was somewhat a burden to the place and the world as a whole. Many of my friends had found a family now. Sometimes, they did send me some food or clothes, which the nuns handed to me, with the cryptic sentence—'came especially for you.'

I had the knack of making people feel sorry for me, which was a gift I had been handed—you can say it was a natural talent. Alas, 'sympathy' does not get you adopted, sympathy does not make people include you in their lives, and sympathy can only just about get you bits and pieces.

However, I did have some usefulness to the nuns. They paraded me before the potential benefactors and that probably managed to convince them enough to earn my place in the orphanage. Maybe, that was why they still had not thrown me out. The orphanage did offer a roof over my head and food in my stomach. What else can one want in the end?

But we humans are weird and our brains weirder. It creates a craving for freedom, the want of love, and the ambition of one's own identity, no matter how insignificant. The feeling of never having enough, someone else always having it better.

It was a manufacturer's defect with no replacement policy. Our own creator has perfectly designed and deceived us humans to strive for more and more. That is why the world is what it is today, for better or worse.

I had become the oldest kid in the orphanage, and all my friends and almost all my counterparts had left. Well almost all, expect Shanti the deaf and dumb, who stood by me and was in fact as old as I was. We spent a lot of time together and often helped the nuns look after the younger ones, grudgingly. The deaf had a somewhat pretty face, unlike my sinister features. It was only when she tried to communicate that people noticed ugliness in her deafness and dumbness. Together we looked like the 'almost beauty' and the 'somewhat beast.'

She too had been in the orphanage since her birth, for reasons best known to her. Her secrets were safely locked behind the doors of her dumbness. The nuns revealed nothing, acknowledged nothing. They were bad in a good way, good in a bad way. They always berated me with their silence and decency, and believe me that is the worst kind.

Living in an orphanage is like waiting for your life to happen. Every day is the same, only you grow older and less wise. With the crowd growing younger and younger every day, you gradually start to feel out of place like a tiger in the zoo. We had been taken to visit the zoo once, and I am sure I saw the tiger give me the look of a prisoner. What am I doing here? I don't belong here, that is what I heard loud and clear. I felt exactly like that tiger. Maybe other tigers were happy in the zoo, but I can vouch for that particular one that I saw, as it definitely felt bonded.

Maybe, people living in their homes surrounded by their loved ones sometimes also feel the same, but I for one cannot vouch for that. I have never known a home, let alone loved ones, whatever it may mean, but I have also seen people with big homes go around with exactly the same look in their eyes. Maybe I am wrong, but I have the responsibility of telling exactly what I feel.

So, I hatched a plan to run away from the orphanage and be reborn to this world. Shanti also wanted to go with me; she too was tired of her present life.

We made our way at exactly midnight—two pairs of legs, tiptoeing silently out of the door of our sanctuary and into the railway station on our way to the big city. Money, borrowed from the purse of a nun, just enough to take us to the city and provide a few easy meals. Two imperfect souls, perfect for each other, hand in hand. One, half-blind, the other fully deaf and dumb, giving each other company, two ears and three eyes for each other.

Of course, there was no hue and cry in the orphanage as no one was looking for us. So much for running away! We could have just walked off with not a care in the world, but we do like to give ourselves some importance, hoping against hope that people will miss us. We did make space for two more lost souls in the orphanage, and that has been our foremost contribution to this good world to date.

We reached the city with high hopes and eyes open, in my case one eye open. Eyes open, in order to look for every opportunity and ears open because they say opportunity knocks only once. So we decided to wait for the knock, our money finished, but the knock never came.

I hoped we did not miss hearing it, as there was only one pair of good listening ears between the two of us. We started to feel the hunger, so we had no choice but to ask some passer-by for money, any amount. Some gave, most didn't, but it was just about enough for half a meal a day, a quarter for her and a quarter for me. It did leave you baffled: you ate but still felt hungry; you ate slower, hoping to make it last longer, but still felt even more hunger. Time or speed does not fill the stomach, the measure does. The food was just about enough to survive but not enough to satisfy. Alas, if only we could train ourselves to be content with just enough. Contentment is a deep word beyond the understanding of most of us, literate or illiterate, rich or poor.

I guess that was when we had already unknowingly started the occupation of begging, but nobody was keeping tab of the exact dates, not me at least. Now, publicly a beggar, we did get some tips here and there from some professionals. The first thing we had to do was to get permission and select a permanent spot for begging. It was a franchise, and we had to give half the amount that we earned as royalty, but a spot, and a few pieces of advice and lots of warnings were thrown in for free.

Finally, as newly legitimate professional beggars, we started our life in the big city. We had ultimately made a mark in the world. Sometimes, at night I still strained my ears for the knock, which somehow seems to be eluding us. I listened hard, only to hear the noisy silence of the city night.

The spot that we chose—to be frank, it had been thrust upon us—was on the pedestrian overbridge in a residential area. The previous franchisee had just completed his act and passed away, opening the spot for us, as if it was our destiny. Timing is everything in life. If only we could somehow enslave time...

It was actually a good spot as lots of people walked through it and there was no traffic to disturb the walker. You also got a good perspective of the locality from the steep elevation. The locality itself was a residential area with as much peace and quiet as is possible in a city. Cows and dogs mingled freely with the humans as if they were related, giving space and respect to each other.

There were numerous clusters of buildings with apartments scattered all along the main road—Vasundhara apartments, Park complex, Hill view homes. A few independent houses were also scattered around, sandwiched and dwarfed by the towering buildings as if shouting them down from above, saying, 'Hey... shorty.'

The steel pedestrian overbridge was located just at the tip of the road taking off from the highway, acting like the gateway to the locality and additionally offering a bird's eye view of the area. It was like a king looking over his kingdom. A perfect place to observe from, without being observed.

From it, you could see the small eateries, fruit vendors, taxis, tuk-tuks, and the movements of people. The police too usually did not disturb us. Later I came to know that they were, in fact, a major part of the franchise—thank God for that—but sometimes they did tell us to 'get lost for a few days,' which we willingly declared as a vacation. Now, a vacation of a beggar is not like your typical vacation—we literally have to disappear. But it did help me and the deaf get some quality time together in isolation.

Begging is as much a profession as any other. We have to be professional. Like anyone, we have fixed working hours, a peak season, and low seasons. There are seasons when the people become charitable, or at the start of the month when some have just received their wages. We have to understand the human psychology and market ourselves properly, sometimes timidly sometimes aggressively and with accurate timing. We too have to compete with other professionals in our field and report to our boss. God help us if we go way below the stipulated target. Some of us have literally lost limbs and other body parts, shedding the extra load to push ourselves faster towards our target.

We also have a very strict dress code and have to pay fees/taxes like anyone else. Lastly, we too are as frustrated with our jobs as anyone of you. So, you see, begging is no different from any other profession. In fact, it is undoubtedly one of the most challenging professions of our times, as nowadays people are certainly not as charitable as before.

I sometimes feel that it is easier to do regular work, but I am not made for regular work; I need the creativity and passion which begging offers. So I guess 'one man's nectar is another man's poison.' Finally, my life was in place; finally, I had found my calling, my identity, and my purpose in life. However, I did still keep my ears open for the knock. Maybe it would come sometime soon.

As years moved ahead, I gained experience and took begging to the next level. I made begging from a profession into an art. I was really getting good at it, and the franchise was happy. I was turning into a revered beggar, a master—master Bhul. Maybe, it was because I had been keeping my ears and eyes open for the knock of opportunity that I learnt the art of begging. I knew exactly whom to ask and what to say. If you tell someone who seems old or very sick, 'may you live a hundred years,' it's a sure winner. If someone is walking with their child, then, 'may he be healthy' or to a young couple, 'may you have a son,' and nine out of ten you will get something.

People are very particular about their children, and that leaves a huge scope for me. Then, there are some people who even if it's the end of the world will not give you a dime. There are people who will actually tell you—being able-bodied you have no business asking for someone else's hard earned money; these you don't waste your time with. You have to know how to differentiate. You have to know what someone loves the most or fears the most and that can make your day.

Then, there are different types of givers. Some give to wash off their sins, some give to show that they are giving, some give just for the sake of giving, some give to keep a distance, very few give out of kindness. As long as I am getting money, my job is well done.

As I was growing in stature in the begging world, I came to know that begging begets special powers. You see, most of the people don't see beggars until you poke them or shout at them. They just walk past you without even a glance. They feel us to be so insignificant that it's like we don't exist. I have heard people talking about their secrets openly near me as if I don't exist; I have seen people do things near me as if I am invisible. If the incidents happen on a regular basis, then logically we must be invisible.

Sometimes, during the summers before the rain starts, we convert the overbridge into our bedroom at night. People visit the overwalk, some for talking, some for taking drugs, and some even to fulfil their natural urges. In fact, sometimes we also fulfil our urges in the night, and I have seen people just walk past, even whole families, as if we did not exist. So, you see, it's either that we are invisible or people just don't want to see the filth around. All the same, it's almost as good as having the powers to be invisible.

I can even tell you what is happening in your house and in your life like a soothsayer. Surprised? A combination of scenes during the night, seen from the high overbridge through the windows, and inference from the garbage of your house, and I can practically tell what you have eaten, who entered the house, who left the house, who was in whose bedroom, who is having their time of the month. I can practically read your whole life.

People are funny. In the dark when they cannot see outside their window, blinded by the brightness inside, they think that the dark world outside cannot see them. I have spooked many residents of the locality by just saying a few words; usually they nervously put money on my plate and walk away hastily with a look on their faces like they have just witnessed a dark miracle. So, you see, we have powers.

Let me try to give to you the feel of the people living in the locality, the people I come across on regular basis. Like anywhere else, they are normal people with normal problems, a combination from across the length and breadth of the country, who are living together in delicate harmony, sharing the same hurdles of life. There are always some people you tend to notice more, either for their righteousness or for their wickedness. Everybody has the trait of both, with one or the other trait dominating a fraction more or in rare cases totally. Yin and yang being the two extremities, with everyone else in between.

There is a rich lady, a lady from whom I have tried to coerce a few paltry rupees and have failed; in fact, she is one of the challenges of my life. I have seen her bargain with the vegetable vendor for amounts that even we beggars snub. When you see her garbage, you will find nearly half of those hard bargained vegetables wasted, lying in the bin like corpses. I guess she is the one to whom the idiom 'penny wise, pound foolish' applies. She is known as Mrs. Thakur. She lives alone on the money that her husband sends to her from Dubai. She is someone who can be labelled as 'stinking rich' and has the ability to showcase her riches. She wears at least a few kilos of gold and walks around like she has just bought the world.

She lives alone in one of the independent houses with a husband who dutifully visits her once a year. I have heard that she prefers her solitude to the city of Dubai or the company of her husband. I am the only one with the secret knowledge of whose company she prefers, especially from late night to early dawn. The gentleman then, in semi-darkness, steals away from her house as if going for a regular morning jog. I am a late sleeper and an early riser; I like to see the real-life drama unfold. There is a lot of drama in the lives of respectable people. It beats celluloid any day and it's totally free of cost.

Then, there is the Sardar family, who own an apartment in one of the complexes. The family comprises of Mr. Singh, his wife, and his seven-year-old son. They own a small garage a few kilometres into the highway. A happy and lively family they are, accompanied by a din that follows them wherever they go. If you hear laughter, 'The Singhs' are in the environs. A very important client of mine, they know how to give. Mr. Singh, on many occasions, has even stopped to talk to me, and along with his money has shared a few laughs with me. He is what I can call a person with no hang-ups.

Mrs. Singh on the other hand always has a five rupees note whenever she takes the overbridge, quietly handing the money to Shanti with a smile. Twice a year, she brings us clothes, clothes that have outgrown their use, washed and packed respectfully for us. That Mrs. Singh has a heart as big as her huge frame. The

Singhs make us feel like humans, the greatest gift anyone can give you. It's a gift that the 'haves' will not appreciate. For them, being human is just a biological reality, but for some of us, it is the toughest thing in the world.

Anand and Smriti, a newly wedded couple, live in a single bedroom flat towards the end of the locality. They have both gone against their families and eloped. Caste difference, the novel caste system of today's world—rich and poor, was the reason for their eloping. Here, in their own small world, they have made a beautiful life for themselves. They both go to the office and come back together; I think they probably work in the same place.

They sometimes come to the overbridge during the night to catch some cool air. They are as refreshing as the breeze itself, oozing love and dreams at the start of their lives together and still untouched by the monotony of life, the world still looking perfect. They talk until the wee hours of the morning, not minding our presence. They can talk for hours about small inconsequential things. It's not about what they are talking about; for them, it's about talking to each other.

Other times they just enjoy the comfortable silence between them, just standing together for hours, enjoying each other's presence. I know a great deal about their lives and their dreams, and it fills my heart with hope. Sometimes, they bring two extra cups of coffee and hand it to us without a word. Four souls, enjoying a cup of coffee under the starry sky, separated by status but united by life, sipping in harmony silently; no need to say anything more.

Then there is Hari, the bully. He lives alone in a flat and leaves the locality on his bike every morning. He works in a gym or somewhere like that. He is the only one who instead of giving, takes from us, snatching the coins and notes from our plate, with a smirk on his face. I think he feels that he scares me, but I just let him be. He is scared of himself. He is rich but has some sadistic trait that has developed over the years, maybe during the days of attention seeking from busy parents. I sometimes want to shake him until he realizes how lucky he has been.

I guess life is but an enigma, everyone attempting to solve it differently. Almost all the residents avoid Hari, except for a group of boys whose job is just to waste their lives by troubling people. Every locality has one, a spoilt brat who slowly increases the gravity of his deeds until one day the deeds catch up with him. He does come to the overbridge sometimes to cry alone and other times with his cronies to smoke grass and laugh aloud. To be fair, occasionally he does let me take a few drags. Drags that make the world look liveable.

Sometimes at night, I go to check the garbage bins sprinkled around the locality. I go after midnight in the dark, after all the lights are off, so that the respectable people may not see a scavenger in their midst. I learnt that I could fulfil half my needs from the garbage bins of the hard bargaining, quintessentially Indian people. Shanti and I have had wonderful meals, courtesy of the bin. We have added many items to decorate our small shack located just a stone's throw away from the bridge, courtesy of the bin. Being dumb, Shanti has been an amazing partner until now, and we are happy in our world. We have made a pretty good life for ourselves, even though I still keep a strong vigil for the knock, the elusive knock.

One sunny day, Mrs. Thakur took the overbridge after alighting from a taxi. As she approached us, she looked at Shanti and said, 'what a rag.' Now being deaf, she did not hear anything. I told Mrs. Thakur that she was a rag herself, what with all that gold hanging like rags. She shouted at me, and I shouted at her. The growing crowd thoroughly enjoyed the show. So I put in more performance and told her that I wanted to cut her throat with a big knife. She too showed the same desire. We kept on shouting at each other until a security guard came and ended the show. This neither was the first time that we had quarrelled nor was it the last. We both enjoyed the show, taking out our frustrations on each other. Then she took out a hundred rupee note, threw it on my face, and walked off. I felt that I had ultimately won the battle; a hundred is a hundred no matter how one gets it.

I have been bantering for too long and deviating from my story. As I was telling you, Shanti and I had a good thing going on, and we were happy, more than you can imagine. We had it going well until one day, I think it was nearing Christmas, Mrs. Thakur was murdered.

That day, as usual, I got up early and took a survey of the locality. As usual, I saw the milkman going to each door, greeting grumpy faces. The milkman reached Mrs. Thakur's house and after a while came out running as if spooked by a ghost, his face pale. Not that I have actually seen a ghost; I have seen ghost-like people and monster-like ones too, but I am sure actual ghosts don't live in the city. I guess it's too polluted for them. If I could fly around, I too would definitely choose the hills or the forests or maybe even Switzerland rather than a grimy city.

After some time, the police came and brought a body out of the house amidst the growing crowd. The police took the body in an ambulance, and that was the end of 'penny wise, pound foolish.' All the savings in the world, all the gold in the world didn't help her this time. Her throat had been slit and her house looted, I am sure, for the same things that she used to showcase.

After a few days, the police came once again, this time to our shack, started turning the place upside down, and took my fingerprints. Shanti and I were having a day off and just lazing around enjoying the day, and the police had to spoil it for us. The next day the police arrested me for the murder.

Now, I had been blamed for many things in my life, even for being too ugly, but for murder, it was the first time. It shakes your insides like never before. You hear the words, but it takes a while for it to register. Murder... to kill another human. I have never killed anything in my life, let alone a human, except of course that cursed chicken in the orphanage.

Shanti looked dumbstruck when the police handcuffed me and took me away in a jeep. She chased after the jeep as far as her legs could carry on, her eyes shouting my name as loud as they could. I could see the gathered crowd, some with a look of sympathy and some with the 'I told you so' look. I was shocked. I had felt like murdering the damn lady on many occasions, but then I had also felt like flying on many occasions. That was just a whim and not something to be taken seriously.

No one deserves to die like her: throat slit, alone in her death amidst her gold and diamonds, life dripping away drop by drop, life splattered all around the floor, life fading away while watching someone take all your hard bargained assets, and in the end, by the time it is too late, realizing the importance of living. There was not a soul to bid her adieu in her final seconds, the worst possible death.

Someone to have actually murdered her was beyond my belief; to be blamed for it was, beyond my imagination. I was thinking more about Shanti and how scared she must be without me. All her life, she had always had me beside her. I did the talking for her; in fact, I did almost everything for her. The vision of her running behind the jeep with tears flowing down her cheeks was still vividly clear in my head. She had no one else but me.

In life sometimes there comes a time when you have to go with the flow, with you having no say. This was it for me; it is as if you are in a nightmare, only that you are fully awake, only that you cannot wake up. Everything becomes surreal, the jeep ride, the handcuff, the rough shove, the police uniform, the voices around. As if everything is moving in a slow motion, as if time has halted and yet is simultaneously running out.

The city police station was big and busy and was headed by Inspector Janardhan, who looked every bit as scary as his name. I was told of my rights and that I would be given a lawyer by the state to fight on my behalf. Like I have told you before, I know humans; I can read humans and on many occasions animals too if required. I could feel that everybody had already prejudged that I was the murderer. Of course, the way that I looked also helped; every bit of me looked like a murderer.

I was interrogated and asked repeatedly to confess my crime. Where could I have hidden the gold and money; they discussed intermittently, punching me around as if practising for the next boxing bout. I had no idea whatsoever and told them so and earned many more slaps and kicks. After a few minutes, you stop feeling the pain and there is just numbness.

I asked the constable who came to give me food in my isolated cell, 'Why me? Why...?' He told me that I had been seen hovering outside the victim's house at the time of the murder. Of course, I was hovering around the victim's house, but not only her house. He also told me that they found my fingerprints on the weapon of murder—a *rampuri* knife. What knife! I had never even seen the knife before, let alone wield it for so gruesome a reason.

Whenever Inspector Janardhan felt bored, he interrogated me while I tried to use my power of invisibility, failing miserably in here. This was the case he had been looking for all his life as it flashed all over the media, '*Beggar murders a woman living alone—loot not yet found.*' Every time the case made it to the news, his chest swelled like a puffed up cake, and he started taking on the behaviour of a super cop, like in the movies. Except this was no movie, and my neck was on the line.

Where did they find the murder weapon? I came to know about it through my self-doubting lawyer. It was lying blood-soaked with my prints all over, in the garbage bin just outside her house. Someone had to be blamed, and who better than the nearest beggar, especially with his prints all over the murder weapon.

Shanti was brought to visit me. Like her usual self, she did not say a word; her eyes spoke a language only I could understand. She looked so timid, so scared that even the cops handled her tenderly, and that's saying a lot. She went away a bit reassured after the smile I gave her. She seemed upset but otherwise fine, the best part of our profession was that anyone could do it, and she had had a great teacher. I knew she would survive—at least the thought was reassuring.

'When nothing goes right, just turn left,' I don't know why that thought popped up in my mind. I was at my wit's end. From where did my fingerprints appear on the murder weapon? I tried to recall but had no idea where I had seen the knife before, let alone put my prints on it. Can someone's prints suddenly appear spontaneously? There have been cases of prints of godmen appearing all over. Could the gods themselves be conspiring against me? I never did like that god and his ways, and now I hated him even more. I mean, look at the world, his management is horrible and his timing even worse. One day... one day I am going to settle my scores with him, but hopefully not too soon.

Alone in my cell, I did not know what to do, the room the width of my height really started to close on in me. I missed my open overbridge; I missed my Shanti. I was thinking we had a good thing going, and then this sudden drama had to occur in my life. Had I not had enough dramas in my life? Everything had been finally good, and my life was a success... or so I thought.

Now, success is a relative term and can be defined in many ways. It can mean many things. For some success may be wealth, for some power, for some knowledge, and for a few peace, love, and happiness.

Like I told you, Shanti and my life was a success. Money saved is money earned; if you don't require it, you have earned it. I am not babbling due to the heat in the cell. I mean, I don't have big needs. I don't have a big house, so the cost of running it is savings for me. I don't have kids going to costly schools, I don't need lavish food, I don't need fuel for my car, in fact, I don't have a car, I don't need electricity or appliances, I don't need costly clothes, I don't need to show off. So imagine the savings, and savings are earnings. So relatively, I was rich, happy, and successful.

The hearing of the case started amidst an outcry and media frenzy. I was brought to the court in a jeep surrounded by cops as if I would run away, as if I could. And why should I run away? I had not done anything wrong, and all I had to do was to prove it. As I got down, I could hear the clicking of the cameras, like you see on the TV when a star walks down the red carpet. Click, click, and click everywhere; it made me stand up straight, chest out, stomach in. I checked out the people through the side of my eyes, trying to look casual. My hands were cuffed; I had been given a new shirt and pants. I looked good; as good as I could look. As I was being taken inside, the reporters started to throw questions at me, 'Where is the loot?,' 'How did you kill her?,' 'Where is your wife, is she involved?'

I did not kill her was the only reply they got from me. I quite liked the attention; I had never felt more important. I did not want to think about the consequences.

As I entered the courtroom, I could see my lawyer. He looked in pain as if acknowledging that his client was guilty but he was just doing his job unwillingly, as if the case was already over. 'If you pay peanuts, you will have monkeys working for you,' that is what I felt about him. 'Beggars can't be choosers,' that is what I felt about me. There can be no other situation where these idioms will be more apt.

The procecution lawyer looked like a magician waiting to amaze the crowd. I am sure he was one of the best in the land, and even the police were respectful around him. Mr. Thakur, on the other hand, looked gloomy. Or was it my imagination that under the gloom was relief. To be rid of a wife who preferred seclusion to his company, who preferred the company of the other one. A wife, whose only need from him was his riches. Could it be that he wanted her dead? Could he have somehow made this happen...? Money makes many impossible things possible in this world. He could have hired someone... anything is possible; no one could be trusted.

In fact, anyone could have killed the damn woman. She did not have a dearth of enemies, and wealth creates even more. The butcher Karim across the street could have done it. He is brutal enough. He is used to slitting throats... *Halal.* One time, he had told me that Mrs. Thakur was a witch, and if he could, he would slit her throat. He lives alone as his family is back in the village. He could have sneaked into her house, slit her throat, and hidden the loot.

Or maybe the sneaky Pandit did it. He had access to her house and often entered her house with horoscopes. Mrs. Thakur was a firm believer in astrology, and the bloody fellow took full advantage of it. He could have gotten greedy and planned it. The Pandit was a greedy fellow. He would always tell me, 'You and I are the same; the only difference is that you beg them to give and I make them want to give.' He definitely could have done it... I have seen him walk around during the late hours. There are so many others.

Then again, the damn prints, the damn prints that belong to me.

The Judge entered the room, a human with godly powers—the power to give justice, the power to take away life, the power of God. He was a short stout man, looking like anyone but God.

My life hung in the balance, and only he could decide which way. So I started to pray... to him. I searched the room for my Shanti; she was sitting near the entrance looking at me. Somehow, I felt reassured by her presence. She was there for me even though she would not hear or understand a thing. The case had begun; the fight for my freedom and probably my life had begun.

The prosecution put up the case, pointing out that it was an open-and-shut case and would not take much time. A lady was murdered, a premeditated murder, murder weapon was found, her own knife was found with the defendant's fingerprints. People had seen the two of them argue, the defendant had threatened repeatedly to kill the victim in front of many witnesses, and defendant knew the lady lived alone. He had killed her and hidden the loot.

Now when he put it like that even I believed him, my lawyer more so. A few witnesses had seen me around the garbage bin at around midnight, the murder time.

The witness Hari was called in the witness box. The prosecution asked him to tell clearly what he saw. The witness told that he had just come out to take a walk after dinner and he had indeed seen me around midnight with my hand inside the bin, as if trying to hide something. He also added that sometimes when I was high with marijuana, he had heard me say that I was looking for opportunity...something about a knock of opportunity. He used my words against me. Could he have done it... and then blamed me? But the damn fingerprints... How?

The next witness, Mr. Singh, was also coming back from his garage that day and had been late as his scooter had broken down and he had to walk back home. He too had seen me walking away from the bin. He also added that I was not capable of a murder. He was sharply refuted by the prosecution.

Could Mr. Singh have done it...? You never know; no one can be trusted. My lawyer had nothing substantial to cross-question the witnesses. All he asked was—did they actually see the knife in my hand? The prosecution said that it did not matter, as my fingerprints were clear on the knife, as clear as the sky on a sunny day.

My lawyer put up my side of the story. Yes, I was near the bin at the said time, but I had been doing that for years now to scavenge for food. I had no personal enmity with the lady, barring a few occasional quarrels, but the lady had quarrelled with almost everybody from the locality except the statue of Mahatma Gandhi. Also, the loot had not been found. No one had actually seen me inside the victim's house. It was a weak defence as the finding of my print on the murder weapon had already convicted me.

The arguments from both sides closed. The Judge broke for one hour after which he would give his ruling.

With each passing minute, the short and stout Judge seemed to grow in stature before my eyes. He had indeed become a god to me. My life hung in the balance, and he was holding it, deciding which side was heavier, my survival or my death.

He summarized the whole episode and announced that I was indeed guilty of murdering an innocent, single, and respected lady in such a gruesome manner. Not only that, but I had hidden the loot and refused to divulge its whereabouts. The case was clear as my fingerprints, without any doubt, were found on the weapon of murder. Therefore, by the power granted to him by I think God and under section 302, 303 IPC, not sure of the numbers, I was found guilty and was sentenced to be hanged until I was dead.

By the look on my face, Shanti had come to know the ruling. She turned white as a sheet, about to collapse. I felt like my breath had stopped, and I kept staring at the one person that I had really loved in this life.

I was taken from the courtroom handcuffed and surrounded by police, carving a way through the crowd. Shanti somehow managed to get in front of me and wrapped herself around me, tears flowing freely. The police roughly pulled her away from me. The media people, with their cameras, ran in hordes towards me. The police let Shanti free, and she ran to me again, catching me tightly. I looked into her eyes and told her that I was not a murderer. She believed me; her eyes told me so. That was enough for me.

I told her to go and lead her life and forget about me. She cried, but she knew she had no choice. Numerous cameras captured the whole episode. However, it was like a silent movie. People would be adjusting the volume on their sets later. We both had not uttered a single sound, our eyes did all the talking, and only we could hear each other, only we could understand each other. That was the last time I saw my Shanti, the look on her eyes engraved in my heart for eternity.

I was not worried about myself and had no qualms about my life. But I did worry about Shanti. She would be devastated without me. She had been dependent on me throughout her life, and she loved me in her own quiet way. We had just recently decided to start our own family after much deliberation. The only fear was that our disabilities would be handed down to our children—eyes and beauty from me and ears from her, and tragedy would befall us. We were willing to take a chance on it being the reverse. I was not convinced, but Shanti was not only dumb but also stubborn as hell. Why does life give you a kick when you least expect it, and when you least deserve it?

I was being driven in a prison van, taken from the local jail to the bigger jail where I was to be hanged until death. As we crossed the overbridge, my eyes sought Shanti, my deaf, but someone else had taken our spot. The franchise does not waste time. She must have been so scared that she had run away. Maybe she went back to the safety of the orphanage. I hoped she was safe; a single woman draws as much trouble as light draws moths. I prayed that God at least does his job properly this once. May God protect her and give her happiness.

I was going to see this free world of mine for the last time. I had loved my life; I had enjoyed spending time with Shanti. I had no regrets, nothing to leave behind; I had no one to leave behind except Shanti. A perfect way to die for a man designed to die. The only pain in my heart was that I had been punished for a crime I did not commit, damn those fingerprints.

If only I knew who did it, If only I knew how. I would gladly give my life for the answers to the puzzle. The hanging sentence is very cruel. They do not hang you at once. Time passes, months of time, and you die a thousand deaths waiting for your death.

***

And at last, the day came...

I was taken from my cell towards the gallows amidst a din created by the banging of the mugs against the cell bars, a tribute the prisoners offer to the dead. I was not scared. I did not feel anything. I was just numb everywhere. My legs had turned into jelly. I was held tightly on both sides and dragged up the steps of the gallows. A black hood was put over my head amidst the chanting of a priest. As I got ready to face my creator, suddenly, a thought struck my mind.

If someone put the knife in the bin intentionally after the murder, I could possibly have caught it with my hand while feeling for food in the dark with only one eye. When you feel for food in the dark, your mind is attuned only to see and feel for the soft food, and the hunger gnawing at your stomach does not help, so if you catch a hard knife handle, you involuntarily tend to let it go. No right-minded murderer would leave the weapon of murder so close to the vicinity of the murder site. It was purposely left there for the police to find it with my prints. I was framed.

Only Shanti knew that I would be putting my hand in the bin that night. Only she knew, only she could...

Like I told you, life is funny, and the Almighty has a sadistic sense of humour. Opportunity had knocked, and only the deaf had heard it. She had heard it loud and clear inside her head and had the conviction to answer it.

'Good for her...'

I thought I knew people and could read them like a book. Humans are complex and women even more cryptic. It was my mistake... my Bhul.

THE ARRANGED MARRIAGE

Have you ever tossed a coin to solve your confusion? Have you noticed that when the coin comes down, flipping through the air, your heart already knows the side you want it to be? Sometimes, life is like that. You know what you want but don't have the conviction to say so. You need the coin, be it a friend, family, an acquaintance, or literally a coin.

I toss the coin; up it goes, mocking gravity and flipping my destiny over and over again. It reaches its pinnacle, for a split second it holds on to its position, and then it gives way for gravity to take over. As it speeds back down, I catch the coin in between my spread out palms. I know what I want but destiny's plan is firmly lodged between my hands. Heads I jump, tails I don't, simple but with drastic consequences. I slowly pry my palms apart. Heads, I jump... shit.

I slowly walk over to the balustrade of the terrace of the seven-storied building. I look down. Now, when you look down with the intention that I had, seven stories seems a long way down, a very long way. I start to think—will I get hurt, will it pain? Well, actually, it's quite crazy because I am more scared of heights than death itself. At that moment, foolish thoughts visit your mind. Is this a good way to go—splattered all over the place? Is it dignified enough? I am about to die, and I think about dignity. Is dignity more important than life? Is it why people give their lives for freedom? Is it why people give their lives for their rights? I too was giving up my life for freedom.

I climb up the balustrade, slowly balancing myself. The wind seems to be blowing harder here, or it sure feels that way. I take up my position and look down. I still have a last chance to change my mind, but I firmly believe in destiny. I take a deep breath, gather my courage, and then I put my right leg forward. I hold it for a few seconds and then let go... It feels like flying. The wind rushes past me, and everything is hazy. The seconds feel like hours, and my whole life flashes before my eyes. Suddenly everything is crystal clear, my life makes sense, and living makes sense. I want to stop, I flap my arms and legs, but I continue to fall and then everything feels quiet and calm.... This too makes sense.

I woke up, more confused than ever at this persistent dream. Today was my wedding day; I was to wed a woman selected by my father. Though it had been a vigorous selection process and my wife to be was perfect in all respects, the point was—was she perfect for me? The dream confused me more. Was it my subconscious trying to tell me something, or was it an omen? Was I sacrificing myself to someone who was not worth it, or would it be worth it? It was so confusing. Everything had been decided so fast that I hardly had any time to react.

My father did all the deciding while I stood like a goat about to be sacrificed, bleating alone but no one giving a damn. I was jumping off the building. Or was I? Of course, I tried to oppose my father many times, but who can stop a hurricane blowing away all resistance in its path except the gods, and gods I realized lived in their own world high above with not a care for us mortals down here. Hence, on many occasions, I had thought of punishing my father by jumping. I definitely dreamt of it.

I had always harboured the desire of a love marriage, and I would dream of different ways of wooing my girl. How I would be courting and coming to know the woman of my dreams with romance filled in the air and firecrackers bursting in the background. Yes, that was my dream, my fantasy. Arranged marriage, sadly never formed a part of my fantasy. In fact I was totally against an arranged marriage.

My father, who was from a different school of thought, always told me, "Believe me, boy—there is nothing called love. It's a myth, a dream which slowly fades away. Life makes it fade away, and then everything boils down to convenience and sacrifices."

"What does the old man know? Has he ever fallen in love? I have never seen him look at my mother with love," I used to think, as silently as possible. I had asked my

mother one day, just a casual remark, "Ma, does Pa love you?" She looked at me for a long time, trying to check if I had gone bonkers, but I held on to my question, staring at her, and waiting for an answer.

"Sure..., I think in his own way he does. I have never given it much thought. Love does not need to be advertised. If it's there, it's there, and if you live together long enough, it just happens, only you don't come to know about it," she replied thinking hard, giving back a cryptic answer.

I again asked her, "Do you love Pa?" She stared at me, and this time gave it a serious thought before she replied. "Well, I have given him a child, looked after you all, I have kept his house, I have stood behind him every day, and I have asked for nothing in return. Do you know why I do it? Not because your Papa asks me to... but because I want to do it for him." Saying that she walked off, dreading more probing into her love life by her own son.

What a generation! No one believed in love. Or maybe their definition of love was different. Our generation was different; we lived for love, dreamt of love, and managed to make it much more sophisticated. Anyway, I had to finally settle for the arranged marriage as the invitations were already out, no turning back now if I was to remain in one piece.

I remember the few times that I was allowed to meet my wife to be. My father told me, "We know how to move with times, in our time I would get to see my wife for the first time only during the marriage ceremony. Now your generation wants to meet beforehand and see if you are compatible, whatever that is. So in moving with the times, we have decided to let you both meet."

As if the old man was doing me a great favour. Of course, we had to meet or how else would we decide?

So we had met under the watchful eyes of both our parents. We were made to sit in a room facing each other; she placed between her parents and me between mine. We were told to talk and get to know each other, if it was humanly possible. I mean have you ever tried to be romantic, with your father and father-in-law to be breathing down your neck and hanging on to your every word? They even replied to the little questions we asked each other and even completed our sentences.

Or with your mother suddenly reminiscing your babyhood and explaining the way you used to wet your bed or how stinky your room still is. Both the fathers occasionally coaxing 'ask what you have to ask' as if I was here to ask a shopkeeper to quote his price and bargain in return. Hell, it was much more convenient to dive into a spoonful of water and mercifully drown.

In the end, our parents always ended up having a conversation to confirm their compatibility, and the two of us would just silently sit listening to them. So that was all the meetings we had, the same format repeated a few times more with growing awkwardness between the two of us. I had not even looked at her properly; forget about testing our compatibility. Our parents then concluded on our behalf that we were perfect for each other. Actually, our families were perfect for each other with the same traditional outlook, and hence this day.

So, I set out on a horse—why on a horse I don't even want to know. It's not as comfortable as it looks, and you have to be careful lest you damage your goods. Can you imagine a groom with damaged goods on his wedding night?

The entourage headed towards her house led by a donkey on a horse. The entourage seemed louder and louder, the frenzy increasing in tempo as the destination approached. The crackers made me uneasy, scared that the horse would flee. Now, that would have been a scene—the donkey and the horse fleeing the altar of sacrifice.

Sadly, no such miracle happened as the horse continued her journey unperturbed. I am sure she had led many such expeditions and knew the outcome beforehand. The bastard was only teasing me and she reached me to my destination safely and without any further commotion.

The remaining ceremony moved as per schedule. It was like driving through a tortuous road. You don't know what to expect next. Neither the bride nor the groom is in an actual sense a part of the whole ceremony. The whole ceremony is conducted in a language of our forefathers, which only a select few can comprehend. The couples to be just carry on perfunctorily. There is disorder all around, children running, dancing, eating, quarrelling, fighting and even crying. You don't know what the hell is happening. In the midst of the din, the ceremony continues, like a train on its track.

Before I could get my bearings, the ceremony was over and soon it was time to take my new bride back home. There was lots of crying, and even I had tears in my eyes. Tears for the last moments of my freedom, tears for my lost hope of love, and tears for not having enough courage to rebel.

Now it was all over, and the weeping woman beside me was my wife... for life. Slowly, I resigned myself to the unfolding events.

As we drove back, the nervousness in me increased in proportion to the reducing distance of my home. On the marriage day, the most pressing question on any new groom's mind is the maiden night with your bride. My bride was as good as a stranger to me, and to be suddenly pushed, literally pushed into the room with all your well-wishers behind the door with their ears pressed against it is a tremendous pressure.

That is exactly what happened to me. The question foremost in my mind was—"Will I be able to perform? Will she be satisfied?" I am sure everyone had the same thought on their minds. Those sadist bastards.

Inside the room, I locked the door and immediately spotted a glass of milk. For God's sake, how does milk help? I am sure a glass of whisky certainly would, but a glass of milk, again I don't understand. So, my new bride was sitting on the decorated bed with her head bowed. The rose petals on the bed, danced to the tune of the light breeze of the ceiling fan.

"Good evening, Madam," I said, my voice breaking at the crucial junctures. She looked up at me, shell-shocked. I could swear I heard laughing outside. I wanted to slap myself, many times. What the hell was wrong with me? I moved forward one step at a time, words failing me. I tried to think of what next to say, I got no help from my so-called better half.

"So... how have you been?" I forced myself to say something—anything to break the awkward situation—but I instantly realized the crap coming out of my mouth as soon as it left my lips. Still, there was no answer.

I reached near the bed and did not know whether to sit or stand or simply jump out of the nearest window. Still... no help from her. I was sure that I heard one of my cousins shout from behind the door, "Be a man."

These three words have put many a member of the male fraternity in situations that cannot be fathomed under normal circumstances, and from which one cannot back out easily. I am sure every male agrees that "be a man" is one of the most dangerous sentences in the world.

To be a man is not an easy thing. Nervousness shrivels up your balls to the size of the smallest marbles, and your goods do not seem so good after all—they seem flaccid. I had run out of options, and so the next best thing was to keep still and more importantly keep my mouth shut. I kept still, the silence rapidly taking the shape of extreme awkwardness between the two of us. Suddenly, she spoke in her sweet voice.

"Are you still a bloody virgin?"

The manly groom expects a lot of things from his brand new wife, but to hear "are you still a bloody virgin?" is the least of them. The worst of it was the way she asked the question, accusingly, as if being a virgin was the greatest sin of all. Her words resonated across the room, completely flattening my male ego.

The shrivelling continued, heading towards a new record, and I actually had to check my pants to see if the marbles, in fact, had not totally disappeared for eternity.

"What...?," I managed to ask, to confirm if I had heard it correctly the first time, the question coming out in a hoarse whisper.

"I asked... are you still a bloody virgin?" she repeated the words slowly and very distinctly this time, emphasizing each word as she spoke. I sat down on the edge of the bed, beads of sweat forming on my forehead, which I quickly wiped with the sleeves of my

Sherwani, the traditional coat I was wearing for my wedding.

I tried to work out the appropriate manly answer. I suddenly realized that in such circumstances, you forget about a manly answer. In fact, you are no more "the man" anymore; you are cruelly reduced to the status of a shivering pet puppy.

"What do you mean?" I asked back to grab some extra minutes to catch my breath and some wits, if possible.

She did not say anything... and then she started giggling. Again, your new bride mocking your pureness is the last thing you expect on your wedding night. Now, I was hundred per cent sure that this must be one of those situations in life in which even the gods are taken aback or more appropriately laughing their heads off. The God Almighty definitely has a lousy sense of humour; no wonder the world is as crazy as it is today.

Unlike me, the two of us alone for the first time seemed to have boosted her confidence. The giggling continued, the shrivelling had been completed, and I could now officially not feel my balls anymore. If the earth would have split and swallowed me up right then, I would gladly be the martyr than to hear the continued giggling that mocked my virginity. Now, I understood how Sita must have felt in the Ramayana.

I had to get back in the game and take control of the situation. I picked up the glass of milk and drank it in a gulp. "Are you?" I asked back, trying to shock her too.

"Are you crazy? Which century are you living in?"

Again, the new manly groom expects many things from his wife, but, "Are you crazy? Which century are you living in?" as an answer to the type of question I had put up, is the last thing you want to hear from your new wife, that too on your wedding night.

Her words felt like someone pointing a machine gun at me and then shooting at my heart repeatedly. I was sure that if I checked my goods right now it would surely have completely receded into my belly and gone into hiding. I kept quiet, trying to process the information just received by my brain, but within moments, my brain crashed and I felt numb all over.

So much for the vigorous selection methods of my father, damn him and his arranged marriage and damn him again. This clearly brought to light the fallacy of the selection process of an arranged marriage. How much can you learn about each other within the confines of the eroding traditions?

The situation was now officially out of my control, and I just sat on the edge of the bed, staring blankly at the floor. Within moments, I had become the underdog. I just sat shell-shocked, my body and mind coming to a complete standstill.

"Are you really one?" she queried again, and then added against my silence, "Sooo sweet... sooo cute."

If being a bloody virgin was sweet and cute then I must be the sweetest and the cutest man in the country if not the world, as I had never even had a friend of the opposite sex, let alone have sex. I was truly flabbergasted.

In such a situation what can one do? So once again, in an attempt to regain my lost honour, I said confidently, my chest out, "At least one of us is experienced. Good... now you teach me without any further delay." After all, one has only so much pride to lose.

My bride laughed, and then oozing sympathy, turned me towards her with both her hands, the role reversed.

"I knew it the first time I saw you—that you were not the narrow-minded type, and that is exactly why I agreed to this marriage. Otherwise, in this time and age, arranged marriage is passé," she said, smiling openly at me. I was still a bit confused. Had I won or lost the game?

But who cares? Sympathy or love, it felt good enough for me, and I was falling in love with my wife—she was at least pure of heart. I remembered my friend telling me that virginity was after all an overhyped subject—'big issue over a little tissue.' And boy, did she teach me... What a night it was!

That night, finally I realized that love before the marriage or after the marriage did not matter. As long as there was love in the marriage, it was enough. The damn recurring dream was telling me to take a leap of faith...

THE DYING LAKE

The lake glistened in the sunlight. An occasional gust of wind gave birth to gentle ripples on her surface that radiated and broke against the shores, lovingly. The edges of the lake were just starting to freeze and would be completely frozen by the end of November. The sacred lake stood proudly against the backdrop of snow-capped mountains at an altitude of about 12000 feet. It was just an hour and a half drive from the city, and you gained an elevation of 6500 feet in just that much time; the journey took your breath away, literally.

Trains of tourist jeeps moved uphill along the winding road, their pace checked by the thin air around. Hundreds came in one day, and hordes of tourists enjoyed the serene surroundings away from the hustle and bustle of the cities.

The delicate surroundings seemed somewhat irate by the disturbance, the lake herself screaming, "Leave me alone, let me be," unheard by anyone. Yet, you could hear it, if you listened carefully, if you cared enough. If you stopped for a while, sat on her shores, and really listened to her. Alas, nobody had the time; nobody had the patience.

The day was bright and sunny, but today she was feeling especially low. Lately, the tourist season had started to give her a mild headache and heartache. Occasionally, she would smile when a kid looked at her innocently, mesmerized by her beauty, her smiles visible in the soft ripples if you looked hard enough. But today there were no smiles.

She looked around to see hordes of people swarming about in their thick clothing. Some were sipping tea by the stalls, some were taking horse rides, some were atop yaks taking photographs to be framed for their posterity to see, and some were simply drinking and making merry with loud obnoxious noises.

She especially detested noises. She liked to whisper, she liked the soft whisper of the winds, the whisper of the snowflakes falling over her and embracing her, the whisper of the stars at night. Yes, she liked whispers.

The people came in hordes, gave her a fleeting look, and continued with other activities. For most of them, it was just another frontier conquered, another place visited to boast to their friends and family about. No one actually saw her, felt her, talked to her, or even enjoyed her. It was like people visiting the zoo, not to enjoy the beauty of the animals but to boast that they had seen a tiger. Today, she felt like she was a captive in a zoo.

Literally, a shantytown had blossomed alongside her shores. It had come to life sneakily over the years, a small shack here and a small shack there, but now everything was changing rapidly with the so-called development. She tried hard to think back when it had all started.

In the beginning, she was happy. After centuries of isolation, finally, she was going to have some company. She had thought of many things to say to them, to give them, to teach them. Lately, it had dawned on her that they did not care about her. It looked like they did, but they did not. One day she had noticed a board they had put up. 'No littering,' it said, yet there were numerous empty plastic bottles and other refuse dumped around it, scattered all around. She had laughed after many centuries; she had thought it was a funny joke that someone had pulled off. It was not funny anymore.

Sometimes a group of people would come and collect the litter around, take photos of them doing it, and disappear. Then things would again be back to normal. It was what they called social service.

Social service... she thought that meant doing service to others. She failed to understand how doing service to others would help in the long term. Now, if they were doing it for themselves then it would definitely help. If they felt they were cleaning it for themselves and not for gratification then it would definitely help.

The so-called modern humans were so naïve, so foolish. She had, over the years, tried to tell them, but they simply did not listen. She loved animals—the deer, the horses, and the yak. She could understand them, and they could understand her. They had no ulterior motives, no excesses—survival being their only need. They knew how to live, unlike humans. Humans did not understand the world. They had lots of information but they did not really understand the world. She failed to understand why, why they were so intelligently foolish.

A few years back, she had overheard some people talking. She had remembered it because they had stood at her shore and bowed down to her in respect. She had given them a smile, hoping they would see it. They must have been very important persons, as they wore ties and suits, and they had come in vehicles with red lights with tens of people following them. She had heard of their plans for development and how they were going to facelift the area, build bigger roads, guesthouses and electric stations.

She had tried to tell them that she was happy as it was and that she did not need all those things. She had tried to tell them that her beauty was her purity—the pristine surroundings, the snow, the clear water. They must not have heard it as they simply turned towards her once again, bowed their heads in respect, and walked off, leaving her talking to herself.

She remembered the good old days. She thought about the occasional travellers who used to visit her. Many would come to share their troubles; they would sit by her shore and feel the joys of simply being alive. Some talked to her, others just sat quietly, but they used to understand each other, without the need for words. She had helped many, soothed many pains, and sometimes just understood their silence and held their hands silently with the gentle caress of her waves.

Now, people prayed, they bowed their heads to her, but they did not feel her. She did not want their prayers; she wanted their love, their care, and their understanding.

After every passing year and the tourist season, some peace would prevail for a few months. Initially, it would be enough to heal herself, to cleanse herself, to relax. Nowadays, with so much litter, refuse, waste, and so many activities around her, there was not enough time for her to recuperate. So many things were being dumped inside her that slowly, a cancer was growing within her belly. They were not giving her enough time alone, and these days she had aches, pains, and even mood swings. She had always known to be a cheerful one, but now things were taking their toll.

Today, especially, she was very sad. It was nearing twilight, and the tourists had gone. She stayed still and started thinking. Nature had blessed her with near immortality, but today she realized that she was going to die, be gone for ever. She, who had been granted immortality by the gods, was slowly dying, was being killed by the humans.

She had seen it in the old man's eyes. She knew the old man. Over decades, he had come many times to visit her; they had had many enjoyable moments. Nowadays, that was so rare and every once in a while when the old ones came, her joy knew no bounds. She knew that the old ones were almost all gone; only very few were left. He was one of the few who knew her intimately, who understood her.

He had looked at her with sad eyes, and she had seen drops of tears in the corners of his eyes. It was then that she knew that she was dying. She did not want to die. Her death would mean the death of many. She did not care for herself but for the coming generations. Who would teach them the beauty of life, the beauty of this world? Who would teach them about friendship, about love, about integrity, and about so many things? She had so much to tell, so much to teach, if only one was willing to listen, to learn. Yes, with her, many secrets would die.

She had heard of economics and the need for development and upliftment of the poor and downtrodden. Yes, she felt that was needed, but for that did they have to kill her so mercilessly. The animals understood the necessity of co-existence, why couldn't the humans?